In at the Death

IN AT THE
DEATH

BY
DAVID FROME

WILDSIDE PRESS

IN AT THE DEATH

In at the Death

IN AT THE DEATH

CHAPTER ONE

CURIOUSLY enough, the part of the whole horrible business of the Chiltern murder that returns to plague me, is the part I myself played in its final unravelling. I don't mean that I discovered the murderer, but I was in at the death, so to speak. And the fact is that during the whole course of the inquiry I was never entirely aware of what was actually happening. Clues turned up and were discussed in my presence without my ever having subtlety enough to see where they led. And now when I face myself in the shaving mirror, my chin covered with lather, I regard myself with amazement, and wonder how I could have been so completely fooled.

And certainly I'd never have been absurd enough to get involved in a business so fantastically foreign to my usual well-ordered and sober existence, if I hadn't been in love with Catherine Chiltern since she emerged from the nursery. But that — being in love with Catherine — is one of my big mistakes, and I've got so used to wanting her and knowing I'd never have her that I can afford to be

philosophical about it. I forgave Nelson Scoville
when he married her, and didn't have more than a
little pain — except for her — when I learned that
it was Hartwell Davidson she really loved. She
sent him off to South Africa just before the wedding
— which, I might add, came as a surprise to most
of us who knew her. She had refused Scoville
flatly for over a year, when old Lord Scoville was
making overtures on the subject.

I've known the Chilterns a long time. I'm about
fifty now, just in the prime of life, and I can recall quite clearly that when I was still a "devil" at
Lincoln's Inn Lord Redall sent me with some papers
to Chiltern Hall. He was too heavy and gouty
to stir out himself, although the picturesque stage
of his disturbance that made him the stock figure
in political cartoons came later.

I've known many poor land-owners; most of
our old families that have hung on to their property
are as poor as mice. It's the beer, whisky, and soap
lords that have the fine well-kept places. But I
don't think I ever saw any country place in quite
such a state as Chiltern Hall. It was the most
extraordinary place ! The drive between unclipt
yews was so overgrown that the few visitors to the
place used a footpath to the back of the house.
The gardens that were once as fine as any in England were little better than a jungle, and the cats
they kept about the place, plus the cats that came
for prolonged visits, gave it an air not far from

savage. I shouldn't mind it in the least now, but of course that's all changed and the park is beautifully kept.

Lord Chiltern was thought rather peculiar, but I fancy any peer who suddenly retrenched so drastically would be thought peculiar. In fact, I think he *was* peculiar. You see, the Chilterns were always people of importance. They made a vast fortune under Elizabeth, by a wine monopoly, and built Chiltern Hall by royal grant under James I, and then managed with a dexterity that was significant, I suppose, to weather the storm of the Protectorate and the Restoration. Later they were favorites of Dutch William while they remained friends of Anne, and confidantes of Sarah Duchess of Marlborough. It was said that they were closely concerned with Marlborough and Godolphin's schemes to help the Pretender, and I see no reason for doubting it. They were colorful figures in England's turbulent days, but their color always ran so that it was equally brilliant in all camps.

Then there came one Chiltern who was a sort of summing up of all the other Chilterns. That was Ronald the first lord. They had been offered a peerage in every reign, but they were shrewd enough to see discretion as the better part until George I's reign. Then old Francis Chiltern on his death bed told his son Ronald that peace had come, and as the Chilterns would never have to fly several banners of allegiance again, the time was ripe for a title. Soon after he succeeded, Sir Ronald undertook a delicate mission to Russia for the second George. It seems that missions to Russia have always been delicate. Certainly they are none too robust in this age of open diplomacy. And it seems that Sir Ronald stayed in Russia some years. Being a man of resource as well as delicacy, he became, it appears, the close friend of Catherine II. Of course in England we're broad minded. In fact I don't suppose any nation are more broad minded than we English. But there are some things I think I may rightly say we don't approve of, and I rather believe the personal conduct of the Russian Empress is one of them. But of course I don't wish to judge too harshly of people who haven't our enlightenment.

In any case, Sir Ronald returned in 1764, the grateful and proud possessor of the Muscovy Diamond, the gift of the Empress. It was understood that he had undertaken a delicate mission for *her*; it was rumored that he had been a successful rival of Orloff; indeed, it was breathed that he knew more of the death of Peter II than was proper. But in any case it was known that the great diamond was a royal token of respect for English reserve and English discretion. Be all that as it may. The handsome and discreet Ronald came back to England with one of the famous jewels of the world, was made a baron and entailed his property.

The Chilterns had always been products of their times in one sense or another, and under George III they added their zest to the general scene. The second Lord Chiltern lost £5000 to Charles James Fox at White's one evening, and similar sums to less famous but equally fortunate friends on other occasions. When the fifth lord, a florid gouty old gentleman who wept at the impotence of a generation that could neither drink, fight, nor gamble, was gathered to his fathers and uncles who had done all three excellently, the sixth and present Lord Chiltern spent three days trying to find enough ready money under a mountain of debts to bury him properly.

He was a young man then. I remember my mother describing him as one of the handsomest men in England, and my father's contempt for what he called a woman's evaluation. The situation in which he found himself soon showed that he had more to recommend him than brown hair and a good figure. He bitterly cursed Chiltern blood and Chiltern waste, and threatened to sell the Chiltern diamond. But everyone said he did that because he knew he couldn't. That was one thing no Chiltern would dream of doing. They said that the very life of the Chilterns was ice-bound in the fiery heart of the Muscovy stone. So he

struggled with poverty to ease the estate. He refused all suggestions. Some one offered him the
daughter of the herring knight. He said he was
having no red herrings dragged across his path, and
because the girl happened to have red hair everyone was rather annoyed. My father was, I remember, because his sister had just married the
herring son. But he had black hair.

It was then that everyone decided he was peculiar: to get the estate away from the Jews he went
into retirement instead of going into trade or getting a pension. There's no doubt he set himself
a fearful task nor, in fact, that he was a man of
ingenuity and strength worthy of the ancestor who
had brought home the regal diamond. In fact,
whatever may have been said — and a great deal
was — against the wildness of his forebears, their
marriages, though not always discreet, had always
been fruitful of sound minds in sound bodies, as
the Greeks had it.

Lord Chiltern became — for all of being peculiar — a sober conservative English gentleman.
My father respected him highly and so did Lord
Redall. One thing was clear to everyone, and that
was that the wild strain in the Chilterns had run
out. Lord Chiltern neither gambled nor raced.
Nor did he drink to excess. Then in 1895, when
by appalling parsimony and excellent management
he had brought the estate, still horribly dilapidated
but undiminished, into some sort of working order,

he suddenly showed his blood by marrying a wild French beauty from the Comédie Française. He was then forty years old and hadn't a thing in the world unmortgaged except the diamond.

She went to Chiltern to live in the cobwebby hall with one servant, no company, and no friends. Almost the only person Chiltern ever saw was Dr. Norland the rector, who lived on the neighboring estate. He and Chiltern had been rocked in the same cradle, but he and his wife, a silent English girl, were no company for gay Lady Chiltern. And she found out, it seems, that the diamond really couldn't be sold; and perhaps feeling that adorned by it alone — if indeed she was ever allowed to touch it — she merely advertised her bad bargain, she retired, taking the title with her and leaving behind a daughter three months old.

All the daughters of the Chilterns since the first lord's Russian trip were named Catherine. He named this one accordingly, and set out to forget his brief flyer into life. One morning he read of Lady Chiltern's death in a motor accident at Cannes. Horace, the butler, told me years afterward how his Lordship read and re-read the notice, then carefully cut it out and tossed it into the fire. He was then fifty-three.

That brings me to the time I first met Catherine Chiltern, when she was five. Lord Redall sent me down to Sussex with a sheaf of papers for her father to sign. I well remember what a dainty quaint little thing she was, moving about the great dark hall very quietly but with immense self-possession.

She and her father, with Horace, who was ancient even then, lived in the main portion of the house.   That is, in a part of it — the hall, library, a morning-room and three rooms upstairs.   I don't know where the two servants slept — it must have been somewhere, of course — but the rest of the great mansion, as far as one could see, was shrouded in dust and linen.   They say dealers used to go down there to try to buy the furniture that was in the old rooms to sell to Americans.   But Lord Chiltern drove them off furiously.   He had never sold anything from Chiltern Hall and he was not beginning.   And I'm sure he was quite right.   I don't see why the Americans should have all the Queen Anne furniture in England.   I understand they buy anything, no matter what it is, if it's either old or new.   I'm told it has to be one or the other.

Lord Chiltern managed to send Catherine to school in France for a few years and a distant cousin took her for the Season in London.   But I fancy she didn't have to learn to be a grande dame. It was born in her, or she got it from the portraits of Chiltern ladies in the old gallery.   She probably practised it in the old hall or the Louis XV drawing-room later in the new wing.

Her father had known mine, as I've said, and

also Lord Redall for many years, and he took a liking to me. I was invited down frequently in the summer. I don't think that either of them ever said it in so many words, but I know that I'd not gone there very long before I understood quite definitely that both Catherine and her father planned that she should make a brilliant marriage. That is, of course, financially brilliant. In the old Dutch garden one summer day Catherine — she was seventeen then — said very gravely, "You see, the Chilterns have no son to bring back their fortune, so I must do it." So three years later, when she married Nelson Scoville, the second son of the whisky lord, I thought I understood the brief glance she gave me as she squeezed my hand before leaving the church.

And now to the events I have to tell about. It had been rumored that young Hartwell Davidson had gone to South Africa the week before the wedding with some sort of an understanding with her. In any case, I was a little surprised when I met him at my club five years later (in fact only the day before my story begins) when Catherine was still the most beautiful and exclusive of the younger hostesses in London. We had all thought he had quit London for ever, and here he was back again, tight-jawed and white, looking perfectly ghastly. I wondered about it, knowing how desperate he'd been; and I should, I suppose, have been prepared for the shock I got just as I was sitting down to my kipper one Wednesday morning in late November. Catherine was on the telephone. I can still hear her lovely voice calling hopelessly to me, "Oh, Peter! please come over at once . . . something dreadful . . . my husband. Oh please come!"

I've never cared very much for kippers, and I went at once.

CHAPTER TWO

As MY rooms are in Hans Crescent I think I didn't take more than five minutes in getting to the Scoville house in Moreton Gardens, South Kensington. As I got out of my taxi I saw the drawing-room curtains thrust suddenly into place and before I got to the top step Flora, Catherine's scatter-brain maid, opened the door for me. She was white and trembling and obviously on the point of collapse. I think I may say I've never approved of a display of emotion in any one but in the servant classes such lack of reserve is unpardonable. Even then I fancy I was sharper than necessary when I said, "Come, my girl, pull yourself together and tell your mistress I'm here."

"Oh, sir, it's dreadful, oh, it's dreadful !" she was sobbing brokenly, but she went up stairs quite rapidly. I always think firmness is worth a good deal on such occasions.

I put my hat and stick in the corner. I hadn't worn my overcoat for all that it was the last of November and pretty crisp. I was still in the small reception hall that always impressed me so pleasantly every time I came into Catherine Scoville's house. It was elegantly furnished with a quiet richness that promised worlds for the rest of the house. At that moment Catherine herself came slowly down the stairs. Certainly the ridiculous people who write the gossip in our London dailies are right in all the superlatives they use about her. She looked more lovely than usual coming down toward me in some sort of dark clinging gown. Her face was like a delicate ivory mask, expressionless and almost lifeless except for her beautiful living eyes, full of a myriad conflicting changing lights and shadows. I tried anxiously to read what was in them: was it peace, or grief, or was it stark naked fear that seemed to leap out like a flame and die again, leaving them great wells of emptiness to complete the ivory mask?

She took my hand without a word and drew me into the library that opens off the hall away from the front door.

"My dear, listen." Her lovely husky voice was barely audible but she seemed to gather strength from holding tightly to my hand. I suppose it's a sort of magnetism that affects people that way. "It's Nelson. He's dead. He's shot himself."

She made a futile little gesture and sat down on the sofa.

"Have you called a doctor or the police?" I asked.

"Oh no, no. I didn't call the doctor because I knew he was dead, and I wanted you to come first before the police." Her voice was a little stronger now. "I wanted you to see him, you know; just *see* him."

I nodded.

"But I'd better call the police first," I said. I picked up the telephone and spent the usual interminable time trying to get in touch with the police. Not that they are harder to get than anyone else. Finally I got the Commissioner, whom I know — my firm looks after his affairs — and explained to him what Catherine had told me. He didn't seem particularly excited about it. In fact he was quite normal and even asked me how my cold was getting on. However, he said he'd send someone out and I hung up.

Catherine hadn't moved during all this. I was a little surprised that she took it so terribly. I suppose it was a reaction now that a man was there to take charge. She sat quietly, her long white hands motionless in her lap, completely stunned, and I had to speak twice before she heard me.

"Shall I go up now ?" I asked.

"Oh yes. In his sitting-room," she replied with an effort. "And . . . and you'll tell me if I need to do . . . anything. Or just wait."

I confess I was bewildered and must have shown it, because she added quickly, "Yes; you see I mean, ought I to get some one to . . . to protect me ?"

"But, my dear, I thought . . . you say it is suicide ?"

I believe women are naturally more suspicious and distrustful of duly constituted authority than we are, but I was surprised when she answered a little sharply, "But the police! You know what the police are!"

She stopped, then added more calmly, "I'm sorry. Don't mind me; I'm a wreck. Of course you know best, but it's all so ghastly. You can go upstairs. In his sitting-room — but I told you. And *look* at him!"

She shuddered violently. I did not know what she meant, exactly, but thought best not to question her and so simply nodded and stepped through the open door out into the hall. I can't say what it was, perhaps a sudden movement, perhaps a smothered exclamation; but something made me turn around and look back at her. She was sitting just as I had left her, staring rigidly at the French windows at the end of the room. I went a few steps toward her.

"What is it, Catherine?" I said.

She turned her eyes that instantly, I thought, had shown something of panic in them, to mine.

"Nothing. I was just thinking that . . . that you're quite right. I can't imagine why I thought I should need anyone but the police."

She smiled for the first time that morning, although not too brightly. I went upstairs glad that she was feeling rather better.

The Scoville house is a fairly large affair, that is for a town house. It has a garden at one side of it and at the back. The side plot is flagged, with a fountain in the centre and a few shrubs along the walls, while the back space is laid out in a small formal garden. A porch extends around the two sides of the house, and French windows open from the drawing-room and dining-room onto the side porch, and from the dining-room and library on the back porch. The entrance to the house is from Moreton Gardens some hundred feet from the corner, but there are two garden entrances, one in the intersection of the high walls at the corner, and the other, for the servants, about a hundred feet further along the side wall.

I am familiar with the general economy of the place, partly because my firm drew up the deed of gift when old Lord Scoville presented Catherine with the freehold at her marriage; and also, of course, because I've been a frequent and privileged guest since her residence there.

She and her husband had occupied the first floor. Her sitting-room, bedroom, dressing-room and bath are at the front of the house along the Richmond Road. Her maid's room is on the east side, between Catherine's apartment and her husband's. Nelson Scoville's rooms faced the back garden, and consisted of a sitting-room next to the maid's room, directly over the library, a bedroom, and bath. The bath was also used by the adjoining guest chamber that looks out over both gardens, a room reserved, I believe, for old Lord Chiltern, though he uses it very seldom. He prefers the country, having got used to it, I suppose. Then, of course, he's getting on. He must be seventy now, though he's an extremely vigorous man and looks much younger. In fact, he's an excellent example of what English stock should be.

The other guest rooms are on the second floor. The nursery is also there, although Catherine's young son Ronald — he's just over five — now lives at Chiltern with his nurse and grandfather, whose heir he is. The domestics sleep on the third floor, except Hicks, the furnace man and gardener, who has a room in the basement next to the offices.

Catherine had said her husband was in his sitting-room, and I went straight to it.

I don't know what I expected to see, or if indeed I had actually expected anything, but certainly I was totally unprepared for the ghastly sight that flashed upon me as I opened that door.

Nelson Scoville, in evening clothes, lay sprawled across the mahogany writing table, his eyes staring wildly into nothingness, his hands clutching at empty space. On the table, at his right, a few feet from him, lay a revolver. I think I simply stood there gazing in horror at the scene before me. It was the man's face ! It was a bloated horrid mask, sensual and lascivious. I tried gropingly to associate this awful thing with the Nelson Scoville I had known. Although I had seen him very rarely — he was from home most of the time, and seldom went with his wife to the functions she attended (nor was he often present when she entertained) — I hadn't remembered him as this puffy-jowled creature. I closed my eyes to blot out that loathsome face and turned away. As a matter of fact, I'm afraid I was a little sick; and I now knew why Catherine, Heaven pity her, had told me to look at him.

As I closed the door, she came up the stairway.

She stopped, her hand on the balustrade, and my eyes fell beneath the infinite sadness of her unwavering gaze. She turned slowly and I followed her into her sitting-room. She was the first to break the silence that hung between us like a heavy mantle.

"That is what he was, Peter. That's what I've lived with for five years when I couldn't get away from it. Oh, I know he covered it up. No one guessed. But he didn't try to hide it here."

She stared dry-eyed into the fire that burned silently on the hearth.

"Why did you stay with him, Catherine?" I cried helplessly. "Why didn't you tell some of us, before this? There's the settlement . . ."

She raised her hand.

"It was just because of that. I was afraid; not for myself but for my boy. He threatened to kill him if I did anything."

"Good God, Catherine!" I cried. "What are you saying? Are you mad?"

She shook her head silently. Suddenly we both started; the door bell rang clamorously through the empty house.

"Shall I bring them in here first ?" I asked.

"Do as you think best, Peter," she said. "My father will be here later. I telephoned to him at Chiltern."

CHAPTER THREE

FOUR men from Scotland Yard were waiting in the drawing-room. As I went in, I couldn't help notice particularly one of them because he was obviously a gentleman and obviously at his ease, which the others were decidedly not. He was tall and blond, rather good-looking and, as a matter of fact, exactly like all the other tall, blond, good-looking young Englishmen of the upper classes that one meets.

He stepped forward to meet me. "Mr. Braithwaite," he said cheerfully, quite as though he were not a policeman in a house of bereavement, "the Chief said you'd be here. I'm Inspector Boyd of Scotland Yard."

I bowed a little stiffly, but he went on.

"Will you tell Mrs. Scoville that we're here? The doctor will be along in a few minutes. And I'd like to talk to her as soon as I've seen the body."

I suppose police work hardens people. I admit I felt a certain repugnance at hearing this bright young man refer to that ghastly thing upstairs, that had once been Catherine's husband, as "the body."

I said, "I'll take you up now, and tell Mrs. Scoville you are here," and led the way upstairs. Boyd came behind me, followed by the three stolid policemen, who seemed to move in unison without saying a word. It occurred to me then that this was probably the first of a string of processions that would march up those stairs to what the press (not *The Times* of course) would call "the Death Chamber." I even imagined this bright young man leading them. ("This way, boys, to The Body.") I realized sharply that this business was getting on my nerves, for I make it a point never to imagine anything at all. Facts are what I'm used to and what I like, although I can't say I exactly liked that very ghastly one in the room ahead of us.

I indicated the door and stepped aside. I noticed that for all his aplomb Boyd hesitated an instant on that terrible threshold. Then he went in, followed by the three mutes. They closed the door and I went to notify Catherine.

She was sitting just as I had left her, staring into the fire. She moved her head in assent when I gave her the detective's message and neither of us spoke for some time. At last she broke the silence.

"Forgive me, Peter, but there's nothing to say. I feel as if I'd been shouting at the top of my voice for days and days. Now I'm very tired and empty. Everything has simply stopped and I just don't want to move or speak."

So we sat. I don't know what she was thinking, but I know I was thanking God that she was free again, even if so terrible a thing as this had freed her.

Flora, still badly shaken, her voice hardly above a whisper, announced Inspector Boyd.

"I say, Catherine," he exclaimed to my amazement and horror, "I'm beastly sorry and all that, old girl."

"Thanks, Dickie," she answered, to my utter bewilderment, and held out her hand. "Peter, this is Richard Boyd, Colonel Sir Compton Boyd's son. He's a very good friend — you must help him all you can."

I was considerably astonished, I must admit. Of course, I'd heard something about Boyd's son being in the police force, but if I'd thought about it at all, I'd assumed he was standing on a corner somewhere.

"I know you're pretty low, Catherine," he went on, "but if you'll answer a few questions, I'll try to leave you alone for a while. It's pretty serious, I'm afraid."

"I know it is, but there's nothing we can do, is there?" she returned wearily. "I don't want to seem callous, Dickie, but if he's shot himself, and . . ." She broke off a little hysterically. "Isn't that enough?"

Boyd glanced at her rather curiously, I thought, and said, "Buck up, old girl." He was full of such admonitions, I noticed, but I confess he was more decorous than I'd expected.

He hesitated an instant. Then he drew out a note-book. "When did you see Nelson last, Catherine?" he asked.

"Night before last."   She was quite calm again. "I came up to town a week earlier than I intended and got here in the afternoon. He came about midnight after I was in bed. I didn't expect him for a couple of weeks. He's been abroad, you see."

"You didn't see him yesterday?"

"No. I left in the morning before he was up and was in bed before he came back."

"He didn't dine here?"

"No. You see I only keep the staff here in the winter. Hicks is here all summer, and if I come I bring Flora. She gets my breakfast, and I dine out. Nelson would do the same."

"How long had he been away?"

"Six months, about."

"And you didn't see him his first day back?"

She flushed. "No," she said shortly.

"I'm ghastly sorry, Catherine, to have to be nosey. It's part of my job."

"I know. I'm sorry, but it's rather difficult. Nelson and I weren't very good friends, you know."

Boyd let the matter drop there with more tact than I had anticipated.

"Who was in the house last night?"

"Myself, Flora, and Hicks. No one else."

"Catherine," he continued earnestly, "the doctor says Nelson has been dead about eight hours."

She looked up at him.

"Did you hear nothing at all?"

"I've been thinking of that," she answered slowly, "and I recall hearing a sharp noise. I assumed it was the backfire of a motor-cycle. There's a garage down the Road and we're used to such noises. I suppose it woke me but I didn't think anything of it."

"What time was that?"

"I don't know surely. I should say something after one."

"It was just a single sharp noise?"

"I'm not sure about that at all, Dickie," she replied.

He was busy with the note-book for a few minutes. Then he asked, "Do you know if Nelson had any enemies?"

"Enemies?" Her surprise was evident. "None that I know of. I don't know many of his friends even."

"Had he any trouble recently, then?"

"Not that I know of. He needed money. But that's not recent. Certainly that wouldn't make him shoot himself. He'd have been much more likely to shoot someone else," she added bitterly.

Boyd put his note-book away and looked at her a moment. He seemed to be searching for the easiest way to say something.

"I'm beastly sorry about this, Catherine," he said, after a minute. "I hate to distress you, but I'm afraid there's every probability that Nelson didn't shoot himself."

Her eyes met his and grew wide with terror.

"Dickie!" she whispered. "What do you mean
. . . murdered?"

She stared before her in the silence that followed.
She seemed to be seeing a vast panorama of events
hidden from us. Only her eyes told us that she
was thinking, quickly, urgently.

"Murdered!" she whispered again. "Oh my
God, how funny!"

And she broke into a high hysterical laugh that
made my blood run cold.

We hadn't noticed Flora standing quietly in the
background until she stepped forward.

"Madam needs rest very badly, sir," she said,
speaking to Boyd. "Do you think the doctor
might give her something? A few hours' sleep
will make things so much easier for her." The girl
had lost all traces of her terror and was extremely
level-headed in her devotion to her mistress. Her
efficiency was a blessing in such a moment.

Boyd looked down at the quivering convulsive
figure on the sofa and gravely nodded. He
beckoned to me and I rather reluctantly followed
him into the hall.

"We'll send the doctor in, Mr. Braithwaite.
That girl is quite right about it. None of us can
do anything with her in that state." He went into
Scoville's room and emerged at once with a man
whom I hadn't seen before.

"This is Dr. Philpotts, Mr. Braithwaite," he said shortly. "Will you go in, please, and let me know how she gets on."

We watched him enter Catherine's room. "I'd give a lot, Mr. Braithwaite," Boyd said, staring after him as he closed the door behind him, "to know whether it's the hell that's over, or the hell to come, that's wrecked her. Mm. Yes. I think I'd give an awful lot." He turned and went in Scoville's room, leaving me standing there in the hall without so much as a word.

It's rather queer that one never quite knows what to do in such a circumstance. I glanced around a little self-consciously, and finally decided to go downstairs.

I heard a car stop in front of the house and stepped into the drawing-room to look out of the window. I was disgusted at our police methods to see a small crowd of loiterers already gathered about the place, trying to look over the wall and pointing to the upstairs windows. Like jackals gathering for carrion, though how they knew anything was amiss is hard to say. Instinct, I suppose.

The taxi attracted their attention and they fell back a little as Lord Chiltern, a magnificent tall white-haired figure, stepped out, paid his driver and came up the stairs without so much as seeing them.

"My dear Braithwaite, awfully good of you,

awfully," he murmured, grasping my hand. "Dreadful business. How is Catherine? Where is she?"

"In her room, sir," I said. "The doctor has just been with her and we're trying to get her to sleep."

"Quite right, quite right; but I'll go up," he said. I followed him up the stairs and cautiously opened Catherine's door. The doctor had gone and the room was darkened. Lord Chiltern went straight to his daughter's bed and knelt down siently beside it. I heard a strangled gasp. "Oh, Daddy!" she cried, and flung her arms about the old man's neck, weeping quietly. I closed the door and went back downstairs.

There was a copy of *The Times* in the library, and I sat down to read until someone should come. I'd just got through the leading article when young Boyd came unceremoniously into the room, and began wandering about aimlessly. He finally stopped his prowling and lighting a cigarette dropped into a chair.

"Flora tells me Lord Chiltern's here," he said. "I'd like to see him."

"I'll get him," I said shortly, and went back upstairs. Not that I planned to fetch and carry for him; I didn't want Catherine disturbed. I opened the door softly. He was still kneeling there, holding Catherine's hands in his and crooning to her gently as though she were a baby. She was fast asleep, her face against the white pillow like an ivory camellia. Her father glanced around, then rose and came quietly to the door.

I delivered my message and we went down to meet Boyd.

"She told me you were in charge, Richard," Lord Chiltern said gravely, taking his hand. "I hope there'll be as little disturbance as possible. When did he do it ?"

"What, sir ?" asked Boyd in surprise. They looked at each other a second.

"I'm sorry, sir. I thought Catherine would tell you. It isn't suicide, I'm afraid. It's murder."

Lord Chiltern's astonishment was as great as his daughter's had been.

"Murder ! Why my dear lad, that's not possible ! Catherine telephoned me this morning that he had shot himself."

"Sorry, sir. I think there's no doubt about it. He has two wounds and either of them would have been mortal. We can go into it later, but I'm afraid there's no questioning it."

Lord Chiltern fixed his eye steadily on Boyd. I was interested to see that the young man didn't waver. After a moment he said, "In that case, Boyd, may I ask exactly what my daughter's position is ?"

"I can't say officially, sir, yet," he replied. "But as Catherine's friend I can't see but that it's going to be a difficult one. Of course it's ridiculous to suppose . . ."

He broke off and shrugged his shoulders. Then,

after a moment's pause, his brow contracted in a sober frown and he said, "I wonder, sir, if you'll let me make a suggestion ?"

"Officially or unofficially, Richard ?" Lord Chiltern asked with his grim smile.

"Unofficially. Why don't you get a private man to look into this for you ?"

His lordship's surprise was patent.

"Why ?" he said. "Aren't you — aren't the police — 'looking into it,' as you call it ? Surely they will find the murderer, if it isn't a suicide. What do you mean ?"

"I simply mean, sir, that in the circumstances I should think you'd like someone to watch the business from Catherine's point of view. I might as well tell you, that as far as I can see now, it's likely to be very annoying for her."

"Are you suggesting that Catherine had anything to do with that dastardly outrage ?" Lord Chiltern shouted, his face almost purple with rage.

"Nothing of the sort. I merely say that it would be well to have a good man protecting her interests. My dear sir," he continued earnestly, "consider her position ! As a friend, I know she didn't do it. As a policeman I know that she was in the house, and that they didn't get along, and that — as far as I can see now — there aren't any signs of anyone's breaking in or out of the house. Don't you see she's bound to be suspected, at first, anyway ?"

Lord Chiltern controlled himself with an effort. "I am an Englishman, Boyd," he said. "I have faith in duly constituted authority."

Boyd made a gesture of despair.

"And with reason, sir; but the police are a great machine. They work from the public point of view. I only thought that in the circumstances you might like someone working from Catherine's. I'm sorry if I've offended you. I merely advised you as a friend, not as a policeman."

I had said nothing during this, until now I felt that my position as legal adviser to the family would explain my participation.

"I think Inspector Boyd is right, Lord Chiltern," I said. "Catherine's position is obviously . . . delicate. Surely it needs more personal attention than the police are likely to give it."

"Very well," Lord Chiltern answered shortly. "I have always had the greatest confidence in the police. It is unfortunate that one of their own number should undertake to disabuse my mind of that confidence."

Young Boyd flushed hotly and started to speak, but thinking better of it shrugged his shoulders slightly and lighted a cigarette.

"Do you know anyone, Braithwaite ?"

Lord Chiltern turned to me, ignoring Boyd. I caught the young man's frantic signal and risked the father's displeasure for the daughter's sake.

"I'm sure Mr. Boyd can advise you more wisely," I said. "Whom do you suggest?"

I thought I detected him in a wink, but he said quite soberly, "Major Lewis is the best I know; I've worked with him once or twice. I could get hold of him, if you like, sir?" He turned to Lord Chiltern, who by this time had realized the position, and seemed prepared to make amends quite handsomely.

"Thank you, Richard. I'm deuced sorry I was — er — truculent. You'll understand that I'm a bit upset. Poor little Kitty!"

He turned and walked slowly to the window, and opening it, stepped out onto the porch and drew in a deep breath of the crisp November air.

After a bit Boyd returned from the telephone.

"He'll be right along," he said cheerfully. "He's one of the best. I'll have to cut along now. Will you send him upstairs as soon as he comes? I'll keep things as they are for him."

I waited a little for Lord Chiltern. He remained there in the window, his head sunk on his breast. Realizing that he wanted to be alone, I slipped out of the library into the hall to wait for Major Lewis.

CHAPTER FOUR

I HADN'T waited very long when Major Lewis came. He was a large man, over six feet, I should judge, dressed in rough grey Harris tweeds. I don't as a rule pay much attention to men's faces, but considering the events of the last hour and the purpose of our calling in this man, I studied him with some interest. Boyd had impressed me with the seriousness of Catherine's position, largely by what I felt he'd left unsaid. I therefore felt we were for good or ill, so to speak, in this man's hands.

I thought there was something reassuring about his tanned irregular features. He was not handsome, but he was distinguished looking, to use an abused phrase. He had "manner." He was reserved but not cold; in fact, it was the rather firm kindliness about him that later impressed me most. His blue eyes looked at you steadily and calmly and his voice was that of a cultivated man of the world. He was not at all the sort of person I should have imagined a private enquiry agent, as they call it, to be.

"I should like to go upstairs at once, Mr. Braithwaite," he said, after we had exchanged the usual formalities. "Then I'd like to see Lord Chiltern and Mrs. Scoville."

So, for the second time that morning, which

already seemed a day dim and long forgot, I led the way upstairs. But it was with a better heart than the first time.

"You might come in, Mr. Braithwaite," he said, as I indicated the door and turned to leave. "I like to have a legal mind around, someway." He smiled, but somehow I didn't feel that he meant to be offensive. Not, of course, that I remotely consider the term offensive, quite the contrary; but I believe the lay public universally regard it as such.

He stepped in. Boyd got up from his knees on the floor.

"This way, sir," he said blithely, "if you're hunting scenes for the kiddies' Christmas tableau."

Seeing me he stopped abruptly, but without any of the confusion that I should have expected. Major Lewis said nothing, but merely stood there, one cheek drawn in, and looked around over the terrible room. I could have sworn that not even a thread on the floor escaped his eye, which eventually rested steadily on the covered heap on the floor. Finally he fished about in his pocket, pulled out a pipe and lighted it attentively.

"Hm !" he said.

"Quite !" Boyd replied succinctly. "Everything's pretty much as it was," he continued, "except that." He pointed to the dead man lying on the floor. I was relieved to see they had put a sheet over him. I think most of us like to see bodies covered over.

"He was sitting at the table in that chair, pushed back a little. He was shot twice. Once straight through the forehead. The shot entered the right temple. Old Philpotts says it's still in the cranial vault. The other entered the right side of the heart, from the front. Death was due to internal hæmorrhage."

"Either shot pretty well bound to kill him, I suppose ?" Lewis said questioningly.

"Right. Seems an unnecessary waste of lead, on the face of it," Boyd returned, callously.

"Not necessarily so." Lewis bent over the prostrate figure and examined it closely. "Any idea which was first ?"

"Not sure. You see the chest wound has no powder marks, while the right temple is pretty badly burned. I suggest that he — generic he, my boy, all suspects being male until proved otherwise — shot him at a fair distance, say over there by the door. And then, feeling, perhaps, that he'd not done his job as well as a cautious fellow should, featured a close-up. For good measure or self-protection."

"You mean for fear he could still tell someone who might come in."

Boyd nodded.

"But surely there would be almost as much, or

quite as much, risk in shooting again, to be sure to
rouse everybody, as in leaving a man with an obviously mortal wound."

"Unless, of course," Boyd said quietly, "there
was no one to come to his help in either case."

Lewis nodded at that. "You figure it was someone he knew ?"

He saw Boyd look my way a little cautiously.

"We can go into that later," he added, again examining the dead face intently.

"Hardly do for the cover of the *Girl's Own*,"
Boyd remarked, as he covered it up with the sheet.

While I felt his remark not in keeping with the
gravity of the situation, and indeed came later to
await his comments with positive trepidation, I
have to admit that they were always quite pertinent, and often remarkably trenchant, although
invariably lacking in any respect. I think the
only persons I ever heard him speak of with any
degree of solemnity were his "Chief" and Major
Lewis. I may as well add that quite unconsciously, I think, one tended to adopt his estimate
of them. I suppose their very uniqueness accounts for it.

Major Lewis began a minute inspection of the
apartment. He moved about silently, examining
the floor and the velvet carpet, the chairs, book-
cases, fireplace, and cabinets. He looked out
through the window that opens on the back gardens. Then he stepped back and pulled the cur-

tains together with lightning rapidity. I could
not have believed he could move so quickly and
silently. He adjusted the curtains with some care,
and a thoughtful half-frown puckered his forehead. Then, leaving the windows, he stepped into
the bedroom. We heard him trying the bolted
door that leads into the guestroom to the right. I
judged he was examining the place pretty thoroughly, from the clink of bottles and jars and the
slamming of the door of Scoville's medicine cabinet. Then he came back into the sitting-room
and stood in front of the table. He was examining a blue tooth-powder box, which he slipped
into his pocket without comment.

"He used this writing table as a desk, I suppose,"
he said then, looking carefully at it. "Doesn't
seem to have had much correspondence here. Did
he have an office?"

"Not that I ever heard of," Boyd answered, and
I denied any knowledge of such a place. "I'm
afraid Scoville didn't have much taste for business
of any sort," I added.

"That's where the revolver was?" Lewis pointed
to the chalked outline on the left of the table.
"Close to his right hand, pointing away from him,
eh? I suppose you're having it done for prints."

Boyd nodded. After a little Major Lewis
straightened up, and said seriously, "Yes, Richard,
I suspect you're right, though I rather had hoped
you weren't. He was murdered, I should say, bar-

ring further evidence. A left-handed man would probably not shoot himself with his right hand."

We looked at him in astonishment. "Left-handed?" Boyd said.

"I judge so. His inkwell is on the left side of the table. The left side of the blotting pad, which is quite fresh, is slightly rubbed, and the under part of his left coat-sleeve shows some green fuzz. From which, by the way, I judge he was writing last night. We might find something about, I should think. Also there is a discoloration of the middle finger of his left hand. His pen may leak, or perhaps he was writing for some little time. He doesn't write a lot. If he did the skin would be rather horny — as it is it's only discolored slightly. Also, there's a typewriter in the corner."

"Do you know if that's right, Mr. Braithwaite?" said Boyd. "That Scoville was left-handed, I mean."

"I shouldn't have thought of it," I answered, "but now I recall that it is so."

"In that case, whoever shot him couldn't really have known him very well. If he really hoped to make it look like suicide," Boyd added suddenly.

Lewis smiled faintly. "Better not be too enthusiastic, my boy. He may only have forgot it. You can't tell. Or . . . or anything you like."

"Ah, quite so," Boyd agreed vacantly.

"Then let's get along and see Lord Chiltern. You'll let me have your data about the prints,

Richard ?   Or shall I send for a photographer ?"

"Don't talk rot," Boyd returned. "I hope to profit, you old ass. Or are you reserving your powers, so to speak ?"

"I've never been an accessory before, during, or after such a fact as that, Richard," Major Lewis remarked, gravely looking down at that ignominious heap on the floor.

Lord Chiltern was sitting by the fire that Hicks had lighted in the library. Boyd had gone off somewhere after a few hurried words with Lewis on our way down that were out of my hearing. I presented Major Lewis.

"I should like to get down to it at once, Lord Chiltern," he said. "We have a better chance if we get a quick start. Your daughter is still asleep and we won't disturb her any more than we have to in the circumstances."

"Thank you," Lord Chiltern replied. "I needn't say · anything about how this horrible business strikes us.   All we wish to do is find the murderer." His jaws were set grimly and his eyes flashed beneath his heavy white brows. "What do you wish to know ?"

"Whatever you know about the matter, sir."

"Then let me see.   My daughter and my grandson, Ronald, have been at Chiltern since last April. Scoville went abroad at the same time. The day before yesterday — Monday — my daughter and her maid came up to get this house ready for the winter. She planned to employ the staff and return to Chiltern for the week-end. This morning, shortly after nine o'clock, she called me on the telephone and told me this had happened. She said he had killed himself. She was almost frantic. I told her to get in touch with Braithwaite and that I'd be up on the next train. I caught the 9:20 fast train and arrived a few minutes before Boyd spoke to you. I was thunder-struck, sir, when Boyd said it was murder."

"But not when Mrs. Scoville said it was suicide?" Lewis asked.

Lord Chiltern considered the question for a moment. "No," he said then. "I don't remember that I was."

"Had you expected it in any way?"

"No. But I didn't care about that, I suppose. I had no use for my daughter's husband, sir. He was a cad and a blackguard."

He paused a moment, then added more calmly, "I fancy, had I stopped to think of it I should have been more surprised at such a cur having courage enough to kill himself, than that some of the offal he associates with should have killed him."

His tone had risen to such vehemence that I was alarmed. Major Lewis regarded him calmly but, I saw, with some interest. "Who are his friends you have in mind?" he asked. "Associates, if you prefer."

"I have only heard rumors of them. I heard yesterday he'd been abroad with Dwight Morgan, Colonel Morgan's son who forged his uncle's name and cheated at cards. Then there's a dancer, Mimi something, and the crew she runs with. That's a sample of them. My daughter's marriage, sir, has simply been a degrading spectacle, and I'm glad, sir, that the man is dead!"

His voice had risen again to a tone of intense anger and hatred. Major Lewis continued to look placidly at him; and suddenly we heard the harsh jangling of a telephone bell.

We all listened as if it were a new and extraordinary thing. Indeed, it seemed so especially when Flora appeared startled and pale-faced at the hall door.

"It's *his* telephone," she whispered, quite as though the person calling could overhear her. "It's in his room. What shall I do?"

I looked at Lewis and saw that he was looking at her intently.

"I'll answer it," he said calmly, and went out. He must have gone up the stairs four or more at a time; certainly it was hardly five seconds before the bell stopped ringing. In a little time he came down again.

"One of the associates, Lord Chiltern," he explained with a flicker of a smile. "Mimi, I gathered, to be precise."

"Why should she call him now ?" I cried.

"Come, come, Mr. Braithwaite," he said. "How should she know he's dead ?"

Another voice broke in. "How indeed, poor girl ?"

I knew instinctively that young Boyd had returned.

CHAPTER FIVE

A LITTLE later Lord Chiltern went up to see Catherine.

"I'd like to talk to her as soon as I can," Major Lewis explained. "I don't want to disturb her unduly, but I think it's very necessary to get her story at once."

Lord Chiltern nodded. His lips closed more tightly as he left the room. Lewis glanced covertly at Boyd, who was staring stonily into the fire.

"Good Lord," he groaned, after Lord Chiltern had gone; "surely Scoville wasn't so abandoned in profligacy as not to have a spot of whisky in this perishin' house. I've got to have a drink, and maybe two."

Lewis looked at his watch. "Well," he said cheerfully, "the pubs are open. Call in Flora and Hicks as you go out, will you? I want to see them. Some very queer things about this business, Richard."

I volunteered to get them, and went out to ring for Flora. I proceeded to the dining-room, and brought back a bottle of whisky, a siphon, and some glasses.

"Ah, good man," cried Boyd. "I've done you an injustice. Here's to you — here's to Braithwaite, Monk." (That, I should explain, seemed to be his affectionate term for Major Lewis, whom he appeared to have known for a long time.)   And he solemnly drank his toast.

"Shut up," said Lewis. "Here's Flora. Sit down, please, and tell us whatever you know about last night. I defer to you, Richard — officially, anyway."

I was relieved to see that Flora, although there was a glint of anxiety in her eye, seemed more her usual intelligent self.

"How long have you been with Mrs. Scoville, Flora ?" Boyd asked. He was quite pleasant. His manner was certainly not that of the bullying policeman one reads about in the Hyde Park affairs.

"Seven years."

"Do you like your post ?"

"I'd hardly have stayed seven years if I hadn't, sir." I felt she was quite able to look after herself.

"You came from Chiltern with Mrs. Scoville ?"

"Yes."

"When ?"

"Day before yesterday. Monday. We got here about ten o'clock. Madam drove up."

"Was Mr. Scoville here when you came ?"

"No. He came about eleven o'clock that night. We had gone to bed. Hicks got up and unbolted the door for him."

"Was he surprised to find you here ?"

She looked at him quickly.

"I said Hicks let him in. I don't suppose he was surprised. Hicks is always here."

"Did he know your mistress was here ?"

"I don't know."

"Did he see Mrs. Scoville that night ?"

"You'll have to ask her that, sir."

Boyd smiled. "Be careful, my girl. You don't want to imply she'd deceive us, or anything ?"

She shrugged her shoulders.

"Did you see him when he came in ?"

"No."

"Did you see him at all that night ?"

She hesitated a moment. "Yes," she said then.

"When ?"

"About two o'clock."

"Where was it ? Tell us about it."

"He was in the hall outside his sitting-room door. He was looking over the railing into the hall below."

"What was he looking at ?"

"I didn't see. I heard a noise in the hall and got up. I opened my door and saw him."

"Weren't you rather surprised at that ?"

She shrugged again. "No. He kept strange hours and did strange things. One got used to them."

Lewis smiled a little. I noticed that his eyes were steadily on hers. Boyd continued. "Weren't you alarmed, then ?"

She looked up quickly, and again I thought I could see the glint of fear in her eyes.

"You were ?   Why ?"

"Oh, it wasn't that he was up then.   It was the look on his face !   It was horrible, he was making queer noises and grinning."   She shuddered. "Sometimes he looked all right, but sometimes he looked perfectly mad !"

"Was he dressed ?" Boyd went on, after a pause.

"He had on a dressing-gown, but I could see his shirt-front and white tie, so I knew he'd not gone to bed."

"You don't know what he was watching ?"

"No.   I don't know."

"What do you think it was ?" Lewis asked suddenly.

"I think it was Madam."   She turned slightly to look at him.   Boyd continued his questions.

"Mrs. Scoville ?   I thought you said she'd gone to bed early ?"

"So she had.   But I thought it was her just the same."

"Why did you think so ?"

Again the shrug.   "I don't know.   I didn't see or hear her, if that's what you mean.   But I thought it was."

"What did you do ?"

"I turned on my light and made a little noise. When I looked out again he'd gone in his room and closed the door."

"What did you do then ?"

"There's a stairway out of my room to the bottom floors, and I went down to get Hicks. Then I thought better of it and came back upstairs. I went to Madam's room. She was in there sitting by the fire."

"What did she say ?"

"I didn't speak to her. I just looked in. There's a door from the dressing-room next to mine, into her bedroom. She wasn't there, she was in the sitting-room."

"Was she dressed ?"

"No. She had on her dressing-gown."

"Why didn't you speak to her ?"

She looked at him squarely. After a moment's silence she said, "A servant knows a great deal about her mistress, without wanting to. I knew Madam had a great deal of trouble. I didn't want to make it worse by seeming to know things I hadn't ought to. If she'd wanted me she'd have called."

"Did you see Mr. Scoville yesterday ?"

"Yes. I saw him leave the house a little after noon. I didn't see him again until I went in this morning to take him some tea."

"Do you usually do that ?"

"Lord, no !" she exclaimed, with a shudder. "I'd quit my job if I had to do that."

We looked at her in surprise. She was quite calm about it.

"Why did you take him tea this morning ?"

"Madam told me to. She said she wished him to get up at once. She wanted to speak to him before she went out. That was all."

"Did you hear or see anything during last night?"

"You mean a shot. I heard something. I was fast asleep. It woke me with a start. I jumped up and looked out into the hall. I had that awful picture of the night before in mind, I imagine. But everything was perfectly quiet. I ran into Madam's room."

The girl hesitated just a moment.

"She was in bed. I could see her quite plain. She sleeps with the curtains apart, of course, and it was a fine night. I waited to see if anyone else was disturbed. Then I decided it wasn't anything and went back to bed."

"How long," Lewis asked, "was it before you were out in the hall, after you heard the noise?"

"Oh, it was no time at all," she said. "I mean, I just slipped on a wrap and was right out there in a minute."

"You heard nothing else?"

"No."

"Has anything about the place been disturbed? Plate, or anything of the sort?"

"No. There's a lot of stuff around, too. Madam brought the silver home from the bank Monday. There was nothing wrong. Unless," — she added, with a half-smile, "you count Hicks's putting my broom back in the wrong cupboard."

Lewis smiled, and turned to Boyd. Boyd looked at Lewis, who shook his head.

"Well, that's all for now, my lass," Boyd said then. "Just send Hicks up, will you?"

She turned at the door, it appeared as if with some doubt and perplexity.

"You aren't trying to think Madam had anything to do with it, are you?" she asked, half-defiantly. "Because you're wrong if you are. It's more likely he'd kill her. I heard him threaten her — and the little boy too!"

With that she ran away.

"Exactly what we're trying not to think, my dear," Boyd remarked. "And you're not helping a bit," he added whimsically.

Hicks was an ex-soldier. He certainly hadn't the remotest air of a house-servant. His face was rugged and weatherbeaten, his hair rather like a thatched roof put on inexpertly, and he walked with a slight limp. He was neat enough, and respectful, although, as we found, hardly what would be called communicative. He was forty and unmarried.

He'd been with the Scovilles since they were married. Did he like it? No. He wouldn't have stayed except for the two ladies. They, it seemed, were there in the winter, and that made the life bearable. Who were the two ladies? Why, the mistress and Miss Flora. I may say I don't like such an attitude on the part of servants.

It breaks down the fine English distinction between the classes. Lewis and Boyd, on the contrary, found it amusing, and Boyd actually offered the man a drink, which he accepted, but quite respectfully.

That seemed to make him a little more amenable, and after a bit he became quite talkative.

"When did Mr. Scoville get home ?" Boyd asked.

"About five-and-twenty past eleven Monday night. I'd bolted up the place and put the alarms and gone to bed when he came."

"Did he ask if his wife was here ?"

"Not he. It was like he already knew it. He asked if they was in bed yet."

It seemed that Scoville had remarked that he'd left his man in France, and gone upstairs. Hicks had heard nothing that night. He had, as a matter of remembering it, he said, scowling with the effort, been fair amazed at finding the burglar alarms off Tuesday morning. Nothing seemed to be gone and Madam had been pale like that morning, so he didn't mention it. Poor lady, she had enough to worry her without him. The master had gone out shortly after noon, when he and Miss Flora were having their lunch.

Boyd asked him if he saw Scoville again.

"Oh yes. I waited up till he came in last night about twelve. He can't be depended on to bolt the door, so he has to be waited up for."

"Did you bolt the door, then ?"

"No, sir. He says he would bolt it after the other gentleman left."

We all sat up and stared at him. At least I did.

"Who was the other gentleman, Hicks ?"

"I don't know sir. But he was fair sore. He's never been here before, that I've seen."

"What was he like ?"

"He was tall, and very young-like. About your age, sir."

Lewis promptly reached for his glass and took a long drink, and so did Boyd. I was very glad to see him discomfited.

"He looked like he'd been out of doors a lot, and by his voice it looked like he wasn't mincing matters, so to speak. He said 'I'll keep my things, Scoville, and it won't take long to say what I've got to say.' Something like that. Fair upstanding gentleman, he was. Mr. Scoville says to me I needn't wait up, he'll let the gentleman out, so I went off to bed."

"What did they do ?"

"They went upstairs and I went to bed."

"When did he leave ?"

"Couldn't say."

"You didn't see or hear him go ?"

"No, sir."

"He was a gentleman ?"

"Right, sir, and an upstanding one, as you might say. Which you mightn't about some the master hobbed with."

"Oh ? For instance ?"

"Don't know their names, but I saw him once in a public in Camberwell standing drinks for a couple of low ones. I was visiting a mate of mine whose missus owns the place. She said she didn't know 'em either. But that's part of *her* business."

"And you didn't see him or Mr. Scoville again ?"

"No, sir."

"Were the gentlemen dressed ?" Lewis asked, speaking for the second time.

"Mr. Scoville was, but the other wasn't. He had on a grey suit and a light overcoat. He hadn't no stick nor hat, so far as I could see."

"Well, I think that's all now, Hicks," Boyd said. "You can run along. You might let us know if you can find out anything from that friend of yours whose missus runs the pub."

"Right, sir." Hicks retired.

Boyd turned to Lewis. "Well, so far so good, eh ? How's that for the start, old fellow ?"

"Well, rather circumlocutious, if I may criticize your methods." Lewis yawned and poured himself a drink.

"What would you have done, old hawk ?" Boyd demanded.

"I should have asked Hicks why he shut up so pop at all points past twelve midnight. Why Lady Flora also did. And lastly, I should, if I were you, now ask Mr. Braithwaite to identify the upstanding gentleman, tall and so very young, who came with Scoville last night."

I stared at him in amazement, and flushed miserably, I suppose. And stammered too.

"That's all right, Mr. Braithwaite." He smiled pleasantly at me. "The Americans have a system of psychology they call behaviorism. Don't try to reason about the minds of animals — watch how they act. You should have watched yourself during Hicks's recital."

"It's Hartwell Davidson," I said in some confusion. "At least, that's who I thought of when he was mentioned."

"Oh dear !" Boyd said in dismay. "Why can't young men keep out of this sort of thing ?"

"Know him, do you ?" Lewis remarked. "Who is he ?"

Boyd grinned. "That you can get from your fair client, my boy, while I go round him up."

CHAPTER SIX

MAJOR LEWIS was carefully filling his pipe and I was sitting there after Boyd's hurried departure, getting a little annoyed at his lack of industry. We were still sitting when Flora came in; no doubt would be yet if she hadn't. That was my thought at the time. I should say that later I realized that Major Lewis was an exceedingly active man and spent very little, if any, time uselessly.

Flora said Catherine preferred to see Major Lewis in her sitting-room. Lewis took no notice of the fact that the girl's eyes and nose were red from crying, which I made a mental note of. We mounted the stairs, Lewis, ahead of me, most annoyingly stopping at about every fourth step to light his pipe. We eventually got to Catherine's room, who, poor girl, looked like Death on a pale horse. Her father presented Major Lewis.

"I have explained to my daughter our reasons for calling you in," he said. "She understands her position, and concurs in my present wishes."

Some people have regarded Lord Chiltern's mode of address as belonging to the old school. I may say I like it. You always know where you are. The slap-dash impressionistic way of speaking always seems to me rather . . . well . . . American.

Major Lewis bowed, muttered something or other, and sat down.

"Mrs. Scoville," he said, "I want you to understand, in the first place, that I am in no way connected with the police. Therefore you must feel free to tell me anything — many things, it may be — that you wouldn't care to tell them, or to have in the public press. It's very often the trifling little details that count, if they're properly placed. And, in fact, I must tell you also that unless you do feel free to tell me everything about this business, without reservation, I shall feel free to resign the case at any time."

He paused here for a moment. Catherine looked at him composedly.

"And in the second place," he went on, "and this may sound uselessly formal and terrifying to you, the results of my inquiries, if they should lead to the murderer, must be placed in the hands of the police. You quite understand that, I think?"

"Yes," she replied quietly. "I understand both of your warnings."

I thought I felt the tiniest antagonism in her voice but Lewis did not notice it.

"I've seen Flora and Hicks," he went on. "Flora has told you what she told us and I hope you will fill in the gaps she's left."

That, I thought, was sheer guess-work, as Flora had not said anything of it. Apparently it was correct.

"Did she tell you she'd told me?" Catherine asked, rather sharply. Women can't be expected to control their emotions entirely, I suppose.

"No. But she's devoted to you. She felt that what she'd told us might make it difficult for you. She was afraid of the consequences, so told you at once of it, and then came down weeping. A very loyal young woman, Mrs. Scoville."

Catherine smiled. "You're quite right, Major Lewis. She did tell me, and she is quite upset about it."

"Then will you tell us yourself what happened on Monday, and afterwards, until this morning?"

Catherine's story, which I shorten considerably, agreed in all particulars, of course, with those of Flora and Hicks. She had come up from Chiltern, and gone to bed early after a tiring day, as they had said. About 2:30 she thought she had heard a noise and went down stairs to see about it. She had taken her revolver. She pointed to a small automatic on the table. She had seen no one and had returned. No, she hadn't seen her husband. Flora's story was undoubtedly true, because she was always dependable but her interpretation was wrong. She had returned to her room and sat for a while by the dying fire in case she heard anything again. Hearing nothing else, she had gone to bed.

The next morning (Tuesday) she learned that her husband was at home but had not seen him. She went out, continued her shopping, lunched, had tea with friends in Park Lane, came home, dressed, and dined with other friends in Grosvenor Square. She got home at 10:30 or so and went to bed. She was not very well, and tired easily, although she slept soundly at night.

A sharp noise had disturbed her, and she had looked at an illuminated clock over her bed. It was about 2:00 o'clock. She had listened, but hearing nothing further had assumed it was the noise of a motor-cycle — a frequent occurrence, there being a garage in the next square — and had gone to sleep.

"You didn't feel it necessary to investigate, as you did the night before ?" Lewis asked.

She hesitated. "No, I didn't. If I'd heard anything further I should have done so, but as I say we often hear such noises at night and disregard them."

"Now for this morning," Lewis said.

"I wanted to speak to my husband about some business before I left the house, and sent Flora to wake him. His man didn't come home with him. She brought this news and I called Father and Mr. Braithwaite."

"That is all you have to tell me ?" Lewis asked. He looked steadily at her.

"That is all there is," she said. I tactfully rose to go. We were tiring her out.

"Just one moment, if we may, Mrs. Scoville ?" Lewis asked. "I should like to ask you a question or two."

"Certainly."

"Were you and your husband not on good terms?"

"No. We had few interests and few friends in common. We had agreed to go our separate ways." She answered calmly, although her face seemed rather paler.

"Do you know anything about any of his friendships?"

"I know about as much as everyone else in London knows." Her voice was bitter and as cold as ice.

"What I am clumsily trying to get at, Mrs. Scoville, is if you know Miss Mimi Dean?"

"Please don't try to be kind," she said curtly. "Yes. I know about Miss Dean, and about other women before her. If he had lived, I would have known about still others after her."

"Then, Mrs. Scoville, why didn't you divorce him?"

His voice had a quality that seemed to demand attention and obedience. We all forgot that this man's right to question her had come from ourselves, and that we were paying him for this sort of insolence.

"I don't know," she answered slowly, after a time.

Lord Chiltern moved impatiently. Lewis continued unperturbed. "I think you do, if you'll pardon me," he said quietly. "May I suggest, Mrs.

Scoville, that there was some very strong reason to make you, a proud independent woman, suffer so shamefully without taking the means at hand to free yourself?"

She didn't answer, simply stared at him as he went on gently.

"I suggest, Mrs. Scoville, that that reason is your son? Your husband had threatened, we're told, to kill both you and your child, if you attempted to divorce him."

Her eyes were wild now, but she nodded dumbly.

"One more thing, Mrs. Scoville. The child . . ."

"Stop, stop!" she said suddenly, raising her hands to her face. "Oh, stop, stop!"

I EXPECTED Lord Chiltern to be in a towering rage at this treatment of his daughter. Quite the contrary. He followed us, after a few moments, into the library, his hands clasped behind him, his head bent forward.

Lewis was the first to speak. "I'm sorry, Lord Chiltern, if I seemed in any way precipitate with Mrs. Scoville. I think she can't even yet appreciate the seriousness of her position. I have no doubt that the police will feel justified in detaining her. Unless something turns up, or she is more frank with us, I don't exactly see how I can hope to stop it."

Lord Chiltern seemed to understand the gravity of the situation.

"I shall talk to my daughter when she has recovered," he said. "But you understand, sir, how difficult this is for her. If you will see her again, later this afternoon, she will probably be more reasonable." Only the expression in his eyes, and the lines that seemed to have come over-night, showed how truly worried he was.

"There's one other thing, sir." Major Lewis hesitated thoughtfully. "I have heard of the famous diamond of your family. I suppose it is kept at your home ?"

"No, Major Lewis." Lord Chiltern looked at him with some surprise. "It is at my daughter's bankers."

"Undoubtedly the best place for it," Lewis said. He hesitated again, then added, "I think you will find it desirable to make arrangements for your daughter's meals. I think the police will want her and the two servants to stay in the house for a day or so."

Lord Chiltern regarded him silently, his face slightly flushed.

"I understand you, sir," he said. I could feel that he very correctly resented what he must regard as an unnecessary restraint.

When he went out, Lewis turned to me. "I say, Mr. Braithwaite," he said, "you might come along and have a bite of lunch with me. There are a few things I'd like to ask you."

He noticed my justifiable hesitation, because he smiled and added, "Oh, nothing that you can't tell me with a clear conscience — as the family solicitor. At least, not much. Better to tell me than to tell a jury, at any rate; which is what I hope to stop."

We lunched at his club in Piccadilly — the Odds — and lunched very well, I may say, although I missed the boiled potatoes we have at the Lex. Over our coffee in a secluded corner he came down to business. Even then it seemed rather abrupt.

"Why was Scoville opposed to her divorcing him ?" he asked.

I looked rather blank, I suppose, because he smiled suddenly.

"Let's put it this way. Obviously she would have divorced him if she could. Not for an instant the sort of woman who prefers to ruin her life rather than go through the wretched business of court procedure. I understand they didn't pretend to keep up appearances, even in public. Also the public, his part of it, I mean, seems to know pretty generally the sort that Scoville was.

"But, apparently, there's plenty of evidence for a divorce here. Therefore, there must be some pretty strong reason for her not getting one. Her husband had threatened both her and the child. Now why should he, who plainly had no interest

in either, object so strongly to divorce ? And
question Number 2, why should she give in to him ?

"And furthermore," he added, with a faint
smile, "I suspect you know it."

"I am sure there's no reason for my not telling
you," I said, "especially as I think it must be pretty
pertinent to the present inquiry."   And I told him
about the settlement the late Lord Scoville had
made on his son and Catherine at their marriage.

It was a little unusual, of course, but most of the
things he did were unusual, because he was a very
unusual old gentleman.   In fact, he was no doubt
positively eccentric.   He had quantities of money
and no education.   Consequently he was vastly
interested   in   Education. Established   nursery
schools and adult schools in all his distilleries and
shops, and made all his workers attend.   I've heard
he was even writing a book although that's probably a bit too much.   At any rate, he had a great
deal of money, and the Chilterns had position.
But it wasn't the position that mattered so much
to him, as it was Catherine.   He became exceedingly fond of her just at the time that it was felt,
although there wasn't ever an open breach, that
he wasn't particularly pleased with Nelson.   He
was convinced, I've been told, that the only hope
for his son was marriage with a good woman.
If she could also be beautiful, so much the better.

That's a theory, of course, that's been believed in every generation. I'm not sure I don't hold it myself, although certainly it failed in this instance. It may be the exception that proves the rule, however. At any rate, old Lord Scoville felt his son's salvation lay in Catherine. I think all the arrangements were his doing. Catherine refused to marry Nelson for a while. Everyone thought it was because of young Davidson. But he went off to Africa, and suddenly Catherine gave in, largely to please old Scoville, I think. She was very fond of him. That, and the money.

He knew, of course, that the Chilterns needed it, and needed it pretty badly. He settled £2000 a year on Catherine, £1000 on Nelson. He deeded the town house and a place in Cornwall to Catherine. In his will, which was read at the time, he left £600,000 to Catherine and Scoville jointly, if — and this is where the unusual part comes in, if the rest hasn't been enough so — if after six years of marriage Scoville had given her no reason for wishing to dissolve her marriage with him. That is to say, legal reason, of course; it's hedged about, but it amounts practically to suit for divorce.

He had a theory, apparently, that if two people got on for six years they could continue for life. I don't know how he arrived at the number six. At all events, if Catherine made no attempt to divorce Scoville for six years, she and he share equally in the £600,000.   If, on the other hand, she divorces him, she gets the entire amount.

Major Lewis listened attentively as I outlined these provisions of the will.

"I see," he said thoughtfully.

"A very curious document," I remarked.   "But, as I said, the old lord was a very curious man."

"A very romantic one, certainly," he replied. He thought a moment.   Then he said, "How long have they been married ?"

"Five years," I said.

"Exactly ?"

I thought a moment.   The date of their marriage has always escaped me.   "Not exactly," I said. "Let me see.   It's nearer six, I believe.   Why, next month . . . no, in a couple of weeks . . ." I remembered the date finally.

"I see," Lewis murmured.   He shook his head. "And if Scoville dies ?"

"It all goes to Catherine," I answered, before I realized what he was implying.   He was looking quietly at me.   The terrible truth then dawned on me. I broke into a cold sweat, literally and for the first time in my life.

CHAPTER SEVEN

As WE left the club Lewis stopped to telephone.

"I think, if you've the time, Braithwaite," he said, "we might stop in on Hartwell Davidson and have a little chat with him."

I glanced at him covertly, wondering if his little chat with Davidson would be as devastating as the one he had just had with me.

Davidson was stopping at a hotel in Knightsbridge. He received us coldly. He seemed to think I had directed the police to him, and I hadn't a chance to explain.

"I've heard of you, Major Lewis," he said curtly. He is a tall, good-looking chap, much like Boyd, in fact, with blond hair and blue eyes. They had a dangerous look in them just then. "May I ask what interest you have in me? I've just explained to that sickening Boyd that I hadn't anything to do with the filthy swine's death."

"In that case I don't wonder you're annoyed at all this," Lewis answered amicably. "My purpose is slightly different. I thought you might lend me a hand."

Davidson gave us a most unpleasant look. "Then let's have it," he said shortly.

"Lord Chiltern has asked me to take care of Mrs. Scoville's interests in this business."

"Hired you, you mean."

"Hired me, if you wish." Lewis's good humor seemed indomitable. Nevertheless, I was a little alarmed. "Anyway, I'm trying to prove that Mrs. Scoville did not murder her husband — if you like plain speaking."

"Who says she murdered him?" Davidson shouted. "If that cad Boyd says she did I'll thrash him!"

"If you'll stop being an ass, Mr. Davidson," Lewis said coolly, "we'll get on faster. In the first place, Boyd's a policeman, not a friend of Mrs. Scoville, or of you or anyone else. He has to do his job and he does it damned well. It's perfectly clear to anyone at this point that Mrs. Scoville is naturally the suspected person. The only hopeful thing is that it's almost too clear. Now if you want me to go on, I will. If you don't care whether she goes into the dock or not . . ."

"Oh, for God's sake don't say that," Davidson cried. "She's all I do care about. Sit down and get on with it." He flung himself into a chair.

"Then," Lewis went on, "perhaps you'll tell us the reason of your visit to Moreton Gardens last night."

"Yes. I went to talk to Scoville, that's all. I stayed about half an hour and then left. He let me out himself. I stopped at a coffee stall at the South Kensington station and met a couple of fellows I'd not seen for several years. We had some

coffee, and one of them — his name is Sanderson
— walked back here with me.   You can prove it
by him, but Boyd's probably done it already."

"What time did you leave Scoville ?"

"I don't know what time I left, but I was here
at five minutes past one.   What time did it happen ?"

"Somewhere around 1:30, it seems.   What did
you talk to Scoville about ?"

"I'm damned if I'll tell you."

"Then we're both wasting our time," Lewis replied cheerfully, and before I clearly understood
what was happening we were out of the building.
It seemed to me an abrupt way of doing things.

When we had squeezed ourselves into Lewis's
abominable little two-seater, I remarked that I
was glad the chap had an alibi, for I was very fond
of him, in spite of his late intolerable rudeness.

Lewis looked at me askance and we narrowly escaped slipping under a bus.   "An alibi ?" he said.
"You're too trusting, Braithwaite."

"How so ?" I asked.   "He left the house after
twelve, had coffee, and walked to Knightsbridge
with a friend.   When he got there he went to bed,
soon after one o'clock.   If those facts are verified
by his friend, may I ask if you don't accept that as
an alibi, even if you hadn't the fellow's word for
it ?"

"My dear Braithwaite, think !   He didn't even
say he was in bed after one o'clock: he said he got

home by five minutes after one. No doubt he did. Scoville was murdered by one-thirty at the earliest. This young fellow had all the time in the world to go back to Moreton Gardens, if he wanted to. He could have taken the tube, which is across the street from him, to South Kensington — except that it wouldn't be running at that time of night — or he could have taxied, or he could have walked. Or," he added, noting my dismay at the trap the boy had fallen into, "he could have knocked up the porter at Tattersall's and bought a horse."

I looked at him, startled.

"You can't seriously think he did such a thing as that, Major Lewis ?"

"You can't tell, Mr. Braithwaite. The cunning criminal sticks at nothing."

"My dear sir !" I cried.

"The only thing against it is that if he had done any of those things I suggested, he would have prepared his alibi up to and including half past one o'clock."

I looked at him a little more closely, but he was smoking contentedly and attending to his driving. I was beginning to suspect him of an uncontrollable levity very much like Boyd's.   Although he seemed serious enough when he added, "Unless, of course, he *is* a cunning criminal, and is aware of the distinct and unpleasant odor — I'm speaking figuratively, mind you — of the too nearly perfect alibi. After all, most of us don't prepare alibis for our

unconscious hours in bed. The point is, Braithwaite, you just can't ever tell. That's the bad
thing about it."

The bad thing about facetious people is that one
never can just tell where one is. I was still puz-
zling over this man, and what I had just heard,
when we stopped in Moreton Gardens.

Flora opened the door and said, "He's in the library, sir."

Lewis nodded, and I followed him across the
hall.

Boyd was the only person in the library. He
was comfortably sunk in a deep chair before the
fire. The whisky was beside him and he had a fra-
grant Corona-Corona in his mouth.

"Pardon us if we intrude," Lewis remarked.

"Not at all, my lads. Just reconstructing the
case from the criminal's point of view," he said
elaborately. "Sorry you're too late." He waved
the cigar in the air. "It's the only one left, and
I fear it's been left a long time. Time, however,
as one might say, has only slightly withered it, and
the staleness comes hereafter, when I shall be far
away."

"Shut up," said Lewis calmly. "Tell us what
you've done, if anything."

"Well, my good fellows, I first went to the Hot
Pot Club. God, a night club's a ghastly place just
before noon. It seems that the one and inimitable
Mimi dances there. And last night she and Scoville

had a tiff. She wouldn't see him when he came in about midnight. She was just getting dressed. She comes over from the Century. Her stuff lasts only about half an hour, beginning at 12:30. No, I didn't see her. I saw the patron and the doorman. I suspect him, by the way, of having all my medals I lost last winter."

"You mean your identification disk. Get on."

"*Alors.* Last night, after Scoville had gone, a crazy man came along — not dressed, not even a hat. High state of indignation. Demanded to see Scoville, was refused, gave the doorman a pound note and was led into a private and soundproof anteroom. The doorman didn't hear much. Never listens to clients, members, and so on. But it seems they were there — Scoville and the mad one, Davidson of course — for about five minutes. Scoville has our hero — with my medals — get a taxi. The two were having words, of which he heard 'Thief!' spoken very loudly. And that's all he knows. The manager had the bit about Mimi to add, but he thought her display of temper only the necessary adjunct of the artiste. Which it seems she really is, by the way, and a clever one too.

"To continue. The taxi-driver brought them here. The undressed gent very wroth, as before, Scoville not saying much. He didn't hear what it was all about, though."

"Yes," Lewis answered thoughtfully. "What about friend Davidson's alibi? O. K.?"

"All sound as far as it goes. Sanderson, whom I know quite well, met him at the coffee stall as specified, a bit after 12:30, and walked home with him. He appeared to be greatly upset about something but he didn't say anything about it. They arrived a bit after one, and Sanderson got a taxi and went home. No one at the hotel saw him go out again."

"Anything else?"

"Well, I didn't get to see Mimi. She was out — but not alone. I got your man Tate for you. He's keeping a discreet distance behind her. We'll hear from him when he can get away safely."

"Yes. That all?"

"Good Lord, what more do you want?" Boyd exclaimed. "I work my fingers to the bone for you, and there's all the thanks I get. Men are all alike. The woman always . . ."

Lewis calmly interrupted him. "You might go up and see how Mrs. Scoville is, Braithwaite," he said. "Would you mind? I'll go over the marriage settlement with Boyd. Oh, and wait a bit. Could you arrange with Lord Chiltern to let us see the diamond, at about five o'clock this afternoon? Thanks."

I think one thing about the people who are not used to having things is the light in which they re-

gard valuable properties.   There was Lewis, though
I'm sure I don't know that he's exactly poor.
Anyway, he'd got his mind firmly set, apparently,
on seeing the Muscovy Diamond, and I suppose it
would have been foolish to refuse him.   Lord Chiltern quite agreed and went himself to make the arrangements.

When I came back to the library a rather curious
event had introduced another, and as it chanced,
a most important, actor into our little drama.
Lewis and Boyd were both standing behind the
long curtains, peering cautiously out of the window.

"Strange how bad news travels!" Boyd remarked.   "He's pretending to pick the dead blooms
off his silly chrysanthemums, but watch him.   He
simply can't resist looking at this house steadily.
Who is the simple little fellow ?   Do you know
him, Braithwaite ?"

I stepped closer and looked out.   A gentleman
about my own age, or possibly a little younger, was
assiduously tending his dead plants — a belated attention, from the general appearance of his garden.
Or perhaps it was merely the bedraggled look a
town garden gets when withered vines lie naked
against the smoke-stained walls.   The gentleman
in the next garden, at any rate, in some way looked
strangely irrelevant.

He was a little over middle height, as I am, and
with sandy hair and eyeglasses.   There was noth-

ing particularly distinguished looking about him.
He was, I should say, a typical better class Englishman of middle age; slender, carefully dressed, a little bald. The sort of man who takes his morning
tea and *The Post*. He would like sports in a mild
fashion, preferring, as I do, the victories of Eton
and Cambridge to the centuries of Hobbs and Ham-
mond. He would like women to be women, not
the painted bean-poles we have today, who smoke
when they should be sewing, dance when they
should be sleeping, and fox-trot when they should
be dancing.

"Yes," I said. "I know him. That's Mr. Har-
old Maitland-Rice. I've never met him, but I
know his future father-in-law."

"Ah, he's going in," said Boyd. "I think I'll stop
him."

I don't know whether our neighbor wanted to
avoid Boyd, or if he was really in a hurry. He certainly quickened his step when he saw Boyd step
out onto the porch. He stopped, however, and
came back to the low wall that separates the two
gardens. We couldn't, of course, hear what they
were saying, but it was fairly obvious from his
head shaking, and gestures generally, that he knew
nothing about the business.

Boyd came back into the room.

"If another person tells me," he said, "that he
heard a pop-pop of a motor-bike last night, I'm
going to arrest, try, convict, and hang him on the

spot. As though he could possibly be waked up by a popping out in Richmond Road."

"Did it pop-pop at the same time?" Lewis asked.

"Isn't quite sure. After 1:45 is all he can say. He'd been to a dinner of some society, went home with a friend to see something, the nature of which I didn't quite get, came back at 1:30, went to sleep, was disturbed slightly almost at once, around 1:45 or so. Then he slept like a babe until rosy morn."

"Maitland-Rice?" Lewis murmured. "He's head of the Gore Society of Ornithologists and Oologists."

"Exactly. It was their dinner. And it was an oologist he was going to look at at a friend's home, or a cross-section of one, or however they're done up. As I hate swank of all sorts I pretended not to remember the society's name. Now isn't that strange? If the little man had minded his own business and left his beastly sunflowers until to-morrow, I shouldn't have thought particularly of him. Monk, why don't more people mind their own business?"

"He's been minding ours all morning," Lewis remarked. "I spotted him peering out from behind his curtains when I was looking around the room first thing this morning. He's probably been there since the pop-pop."

That remark, as it happened, was truer than any of us thought.

CHAPTER EIGHT

I THINK that this day was more crowded with events than any other I can remember. At a little after five o'clock, Lord Chiltern and I were admitted to the vaults of William Beacon's Bank in Piccadilly, where we stood about waiting for Lewis. The manager, Mr. Sumner, is a timid, mouse-like little man, and has always stood in awe of Lord Chiltern, and perhaps even more of the Muscovy Diamond, the royal stone shining so splendidly in the darkness of the vaults down beneath him. Whenever it's viewed by any of the numerous people who are everlastingly wanting to look at it for one purpose or another — or no purpose at all — the little man jumps about darting suspicious glances at the very chairs. After the great robbery of the Bank of Wales last year, he told me he hadn't slept well for weeks.

Lord Chiltern was not as gracious as he usually is with such people, and made no effort to relieve the anxiety that I could plainly see on Mr. Sumner's face.

"Ah, there he is," Lord Chiltern said. A boy showed Lewis down the stairs, accompanied by a very Jewish looking person in thick spectacles, who bowed solemnly when he was presented to us, but made no comment of any sort. Nor did Lewis explain him other than as his friend Mr. Kracower. Lord Chiltern accepted him as such quite simply, of course; but I noticed that Sumner looked at him with increasing agitation. Small beads of perspiration stood out on his forehead, which no amount of mopping with a large handkerchief seemed to affect. I became so sorry for the fellow — after all, he had guarded the Muscovy Diamond, so to speak, for fifteen years — that I was about to reassure him quietly, when Lord Chiltern spoke.

"Sumner," he said, with great dignity, "we will look at the diamond now."

Sumner opened the first vault, and stood aside for us to enter. Lord Chiltern extracted the small key from his own pocket and opened the second. He then manipulated the combination of the small safe. The door flew open and revealed a small box, which he took out and handed to Lewis. We stepped back into the outer room; Lewis opened the box. There, lying upon a bed of black suede, flashed and burned the splendid jewel. We stood an instant gazing at it, Lord Chiltern almost reverently. It was the symbol to him of something almost akin to ancestor-worship; he regarded it as a priest does his holy vessels.

Major Lewis held the small casket towards Mr. Kracower, who, carefully refraining from touching the diamond, held a jeweller's microscope to it, and examined it carefully and long.

Lord Chiltern, at first puzzled, was becoming, I saw, slightly impatient, when the Jew raised his head and silently returned the casket to Major Lewis. He glanced at Lord Chiltern and looked inquiringly at Lewis.

"How much is that stone worth, Kracower'?" Lewis said quietly.

Lord Chiltern looked sharply at them; his face flushed with anger and I could see the storm gathering. But before words could come to his lips, Mr. Kracower spoke.

"You were right, my friend," he said calmly. The eloquent shrug of his shoulders expressed at once regret, pity, and admiration. "Still, it is a very pretty thing; it is very pretty. I will make it for you for a hundred guineas."

He shrugged his thick shoulders again, and only then passed his fingers caressingly over the jewel.

Lewis looked silently at Lord Chiltern, who was purple with rage. "The Muscovy Diamond ! A hundred guineas !" He choked with fury.

"Your pardon, sir," Kracower interjected quietly. "This is not the Muscovy Diamond, which I know. That is priceless. I was allowed to see it, years ago. This is a very skillful paste replica of your magnificent jewel."

For a terrible instant I dared not look at Lord Chiltern; and when I did, after a terrible pause, I saw that his face was grey and mottled. He stood there unable to speak, looking from the Jew to

Lewis, and from them to Sumner and myself. And at once the thought came to me that I knew was in his mind: it was not that the stone had gone, for it could be recovered; but who . . . ?

Major Lewis spoke first. "I regret exceedingly that this has happened," he said, "and that I told you of it in such a melodramatic way; but I was afraid it had been done, and I knew of no other way to convince you. We must put this away and see your daughter."

"My daughter !"

Lord Chiltern had aged a dozen years; he barely breathed the word. Lewis gently took his arm and led him up the stairs and out into a waiting motor car. As we went out he spoke quietly to Mr. Sumner, who, reduced almost to the state of the old lord, mechanically followed us.

Lewis ushered him briskly up into the car by Lord Chiltern's side. "Braithwaite and I are engaged elsewhere," he said. "Tell Mrs. Scoville what has happened; and say nothing else to anyone till later."

Sumner nodded painfully and Lord Chiltern did not raise his head as the car went off.

"Now, Braithwaite," Lewis continued calmly, "we've a more important job. I'll run in and 'phone, and be with you in a minute. Get a taxi."

All of this happened in such a slap-dash fashion that I had hailed a taxi and stood waiting by it before I really knew what I was doing. I certainly had had no opportunity to tell Lewis what I thought of his implication that Catherine had stolen the real diamond. I was thinking what I should say to him when he came out, bustled me into the cab, and gave the driver an address in Park Lane.

"My dear sir !" I said, "where are we going in this mad fashion ?"

"Braithwaite," he said solemnly, but with a twinkle in his eye, "we're going to call on Miss Mimi Dean, no less; so you must be careful, very careful."

I protested with some indignation that I was hardly likely to have much to do with a creature who was in all probability a murderess.

"Oh, come, come !" he said. "She's a dancer, not a murderer. At least . . ." He seemed to become thoughtful at that, and I was unable to penetrate his air of concentration until we drew up in Park Lane.

"The little bird has flown to her nest on the wing of a lovely blue Rolls," I heard at my elbow, and turned to stare into the cheerful face of young Boyd.

"Then let's go up," Lewis said. We entered the place, followed by two people, mute and stolid, much like those Boyd had along at Moreton Gardens. Indeed, they may have been the same.

The sumptuous lift, upholstered in apple-green velvet, took us stealthily to an upper floor. We stepped into a long wide corridor, furnished with this modernistic furniture, that goes off in all directions and looks so devilishly uncomfortable. There were some hundreds of palm trees, I judged, standing about, and a fountain was playing in the centre.

"Now how a man on a thousand a year manages this, I don't know," Lewis observed, looking about him with an air of amusement.

"I thought it was Miss Dean we were coming to see," I said.   I dislike to be told one thing and have another happen.

Boyd stopped abruptly.   "Ring for the lift, Monk," he said.   "I told you you'd no right.   The innocent lamb . . ."

"Shut up," said Lewis.   "We'd assumed, perhaps wrongfully, Braithwaite, that Miss Dean doesn't pay her own rent.   Most young actresses of her sort who pay their own rent don't live in Park Lane."

"Or," Boyd interrupted, "at least most young actresses who live in Park Lane don't pay their own rent."

"Be that as it may," Lewis went on, "here we are, and we're wasting time.   This is her suite."

A maid all in violet and lace frills opened the door.   She looked at us a little queerly, but after a word with Boyd let us in.   We sat gingerly enough on the pale green brocade that upholstered the spindly gilt chairs.   The great police boots crushed into the soft green rug.   The room was the very essence of daintiness, as far as I'm a judge. Again I don't know what I expected the young woman to look' like. It wasn't the lovely young blond apparition that suddenly appeared in the door, looking in amused surprise from one of us to the other.

"Hello, darlings !" She laughed gaily and clapped her hands. "Molly, get the gentlemen each a drink."

"Don't bother, Miss Dean," Boyd said gravely. "None of us being long for this world, we can't spend too much of our little span here."

She laughed again, a picture of easy and charming vivacity. "Well, what you've got left, you might spend pleasantly ! Bring the whisky, Molly."

"Sorry !" Boyd cut in firmly. "I must tell you that our mission, so to speak, is rather a delicate one."

"You mean jolly old Nelson. Heard he was ill or something. What'll you have ?" She took the tray from the maid.

"Nelson Scoville is dead," Boyd said sharply.

"Is what ?" She cocked an absurd glance at him.

"Is dead. He was shot last night."

She set the decanter down, staring uncomprehendingly at him and then at Lewis. I could have sworn it was the first she had heard of it. She was completely dismayed.

"Dead? Shot? Oh God, what do you mean?"

She stared almost piteously at us all.

Lewis smiled very callously, I thought. "Yes, Miss Dean," he said pleasantly, "Nelson Scoville is dead. Don't bother to weep, or faint or anything. You've just read all about it in the *Evening Call*, which you bought ten minutes ago at Hyde Park Corner."

As she looked coolly at him the dismay and the piteousness vanished in a second; and then, so suddenly that I fairly jumped, she burst out at him savagely, her lovely blue eyes flashing with fury. "You've been spying on me!" she screamed. "Get out of my house!" I was horrified to see the blond sweetness of a few minutes before so contorted with rage.

"There, there," Boyd said soothingly. "Take a deep breath. Pull yourself together. Have a look at this." He handed her a document. "It's a search warrant, my pretty friend. We'd like to have a little look at your house first, if you don't mind."

The woman was certainly a splendid actress. Only I, for one, hadn't the faintest idea what part of all this was acting. She gave the paper the merest glance, looked at him steadily, and then shrugged her slim silken shoulders. The storm was over, apparently, at least for the time. This, I felt, was the temperament of the artiste that the manager of the Hot Pot Club had mentioned.

Then a tiny smile played about her full red lips. "How did you know I had the paper ?" she asked Lewis, quite cheerfully.

"Partly guesswork," he replied, as cheerfully, "and partly because I'm sitting on it now."

She laughed suddenly at that. "Well, what do you boys want ?"

"Heard a little tale at the Hot Pot Club," Boyd said. "How you refused to speak to Scoville last night, and so on. Like to hear about it."

She said nothing for a while. Her face was again the innocent pink and cream mask of ingenuous beauty. Her clear eyes were wide and innocent. Although I thought I noticed the faintest shadow of something in them when she happened to glance again at Lewis — who, however, was paying almost no attention to her — I certainly should have been inclined to trust her implicitly. I was even a little annoyed at the attitude, almost flippant, which they had adopted. She had, of course, lied about the business of Scoville's death; but I told myself that in similar circumstances I should have probably done the same. I couldn't believe that this dainty little creature, sitting calmly there, was the Mimi Dean I'd heard about. I would like to think that an innocent face means an innocent heart. I was watching her intently, trying to fathom her contradictions and the eternal riddle of the sphynx, when I caught Lewis's gaze fastened on me with a certain fatuous amusement. I unfortunately get very red in such circumstances.

"When did you see Scoville last, please ?" Boyd asked.

"At dinner Monday." Her answer came very readily. "He dined here. Then I went to the theatre. Last night he came around to the Club, but I didn't see him. You seem to know about that."

"Why didn't you ?"

"None of your business," she answered sweetly.

"I see," Boyd said. "Well, what happened to you ? I mean, when did you get home, and so on ?"

"I came with another boy. I was tired and got here early, and went to bed. There you are."

"At what time, please ?"

She looked at Lewis, and murmured, "I'm afraid I don't just know, darling."

"Well," Boyd continued patiently, "tell me this, then. Do you know anybody who might have killed Scoville ? Did he have any enemies ?"

"Ha, ha !" she said. "You sound like one of Edgar Wallace's plays. Why should he have any enemies ?"

Then the merry laughter came to a sudden stop. She looked searchingly from one to the other of them, the expression on her face extraordinarily hard.

"Now why didn't you say that at first? Because if you're looking for people who hated him, you're at the wrong end. *I* didn't hate him. He was happy enough *here*. Try the other side of the triangle, Sherlock Holmes."

The implication was fairly obvious, I thought.

"What do you mean by that, exactly?" Boyd asked.

"You know what I mean, big boy," she replied rather insolently, staring very boldly at him.

Lewis interrupted. "Did you see anyone with Scoville last night?"

"You mean the row at the Club. I didn't see it, but I heard about it. Antoine — that's the doorman — said you'd been there to help him mop up this morning."

"Had Scoville ever mentioned Davidson?" Lewis continued.

"No. Oh, yes, I mean. I told him once not to be so shirty about him. If his wife wanted a fancy man, let her have one. He saw the sense of that and didn't say anything else."

Lewis glanced at Boyd, who rose. "Anything else helpful to tell us, Miss Dean?" he asked. "Not holding out something?"

Miss Dean laughed gaily at that. "Not I, big boy. I'm for the police every time."

"Then you won't mind if we have to look over your place, will you?"

He held up the warrant again. Her eyes hardened suddenly. She was looking at the paper, but I saw that she wasn't reading it. She was thinking intently. After an instant she looked up and smiled provocatively.

"Big boy, I'd do anything for you. For your own sake I hope you're all married men. Molly! Give these boys the freedom of the city."

She collapsed into the cushions on the sofa and rocked with laughter.

Boyd made a sign to his mutes, who had moved off the rug and during all this had been standing silently in the doorway. I had never, naturally, seen a place searched before, and I've sometimes amused myself by thinking of the places in a house where one might hide something if one conceivably had something to hide. I had prided myself mildly on having thought of excellent places. These spots were the first that the two searchers looked at. On top of the window and picture mouldings, behind pictures, in the crevices of the overstuffed furniture; one place after another they went over with amazing dexterity. They left no nook, cranny, or surface unsurveyed. They even examined the gay cluster of crystal flowers on the glass light bowls. When they had finished the drawing-room they proceeded to the rest of the flat, and we heard them now and again as they moved articles around.

"Whatever you're looking for, darlings," Miss Dean said cheerfully, "you won't find it here."

"Then where is it ?" asked Lewis quickly.

She stared at him, her face a little paler.

"Tell me what you're looking for," she replied calmly enough.

"Evidence, evidence, old girl," Boyd said.

"Then you'd better go to the scene of the crime, old dear. And if you'll call off your bloodhounds, I'd like to take a bath. I've got a job, you know; I'm a working girl. By the way" — she pointed to an enamel clock on the mantel — "that comes off. The top I mean. Tell the boys not to pass it over. Bye-bye."

We sat there until the men came in.

"Nothing anywhere, sir, except this," one of them said, holding out a small booklet.

"By Jove, it's a passport," Boyd said with interest. "It's issued last week. Good for all countries, including the Scandinavian. Hm. And aha ! Her name is Mamie Wilson — that's a good one. Now dear me, I hope Mamie isn't leaving us ? The heart of the West End isn't to be so toyed with."

Lewis silenced him, and demanding the passport, looked at it thoughtfully. "I think I'd like to see her again," he said, after some deliberation. "And let's not say anything about this for a while." He rang the bell and asked the maid to call her mistress.

After a little she appeared, in a heavy gold satin dressing-gown. She seated herself without a word on the sofa, and nonchalantly opening a gorgeous box of chocolates on the table beside her, began to nibble a large sweet.

We watched her pantomime silently.

"Well, I say, my dears, as I said, I've got a job," she announced, with some impatience. "I've got to be at the theatre at eight, and I've got to eat first. I can't live on chocolates." She spoke rather insolently. Suddenly she stopped nibbling, and looked in a queer surprised uncertainty at the chocolate in her hand.

"I say ! It hardly seems right to be eating these when he's dead, does it ? He sent them yesterday."

She looked almost frightened for an instant, then shrugged lightly, as if ashamed. "Oh well, we'll all be dead some day, and there'll still be cakes and ale."

Lewis looked at her sharply, and smiled involuntarily. She caught his glance and saluted him drolly with a large wink. Then she calmly continued her munching.

"There's just one other thing, Miss Dean," Lewis said. "You told us a bit ago that Davidson had a row with Scoville last night. But you didn't see him, did you ?"

"Right the first time."

"Then how did you know it was Davidson ? The people at the club don't know him. It wasn't in the papers. How did you find it out ?"

I thought her smile was a trifle forced.

"Clever lad !" she said.   "Of course, how did I ?
Let me see."   Behind her badinage she was thinking desperately.

"In fact," Lewis continued easily, "you *did* see
Scoville again, didn't you ?"

She shrugged again.   "Oh well," she said.
"You'll get it sooner or later.   Yes, I saw him
again.   In fact" — here she looked boldly at Lewis
— "I was there at his house last night.   I was in
the back garden, and I heard a man's voice.   And
then Nelson said 'Come out of it, Davidson, don't
be a bloody fool.'   Or something like that."

Boyd leaned forward.

"At what time was that ?"

She looked at him archly.

"That, big boy, was a little after I went off at
12:20.   I didn't finish my act.   I didn't change,
because I'd changed my mind, you see, and I
wanted to see Scoville.   I drove out in my roadster.
I heard the row, so I hid near the porch and
waited.

"What happened ?   Well, after a bit they were
quiet and I sort of waited around.   I was going in,
when I heard somebody else talking to him.   It
was a woman.   Well, I was about freezing by then,
so I looked at my watch, thinking I'd go home and
see him in the morning.   But it was only a little
after one, and I thought I'd wait.   I couldn't hear
what was being said, but it sounded like an awful

row. I thought I heard something next door. I crept to the door, unlocked it, and went up the service stairs to the hall, and hid in the shadow of the main staircase. I don't know how long I stayed there. I could hear the sound of voices, and then suddenly there was a shot."

"A shot ?" Boyd asked.

"Yes, and then another right after it," she replied quickly.

"What else ?" Lewis said abruptly. I don't know what they thought of this new evidence — to me, at least, quite unsuspected — but I know that my own heart beat faster and faster as she went coolly along.

"Then I heard the door open and close, and in a minute another door close. Then I went out the way I came."

"What time was it then, do you know ?"

"I didn't look. I got here about a quarter to two. It must have been about 1:30 or so."

She absently took another sweet and began nibbling daintily at it. I was under the impression from some of the papers that the slim young modern girls ate nothing but water biscuits and orange juice, but this girl was half through a large box of rich chocolates that had come only the day before. Certainly her figure showed none of the reputed ravages of rich food.

"How did you get into the garden and house, Miss Dean ?" Lewis asked.

"I have the keys," she answered calmly. "One for the back door, one for the garden."

Then she added, "Scoville was always amused at the idea of my coming there at night, with his grand wife across the hall never knowing it. Sometimes he wanted to call her, but I never let him."

A dull flush mounted Boyd's cheek; but Lewis spoke before he said what we all wanted to say.

"Who was the woman with Scoville?"

"I've told you all I know. I didn't see her. I only heard the doors."

"Then it may have been Flora, who sleeps on the same floor," Lewis suggested.

"Surely," she returned promptly, but with a derisive smile. "Of course, it must have been Flora. The poor devil of a maid, I suppose."

Lewis paid no attention to her manner. "Thank you, Miss Dean," he said urbanely. "May I use your 'phone before we go? I'll need the directory, too, please."

"Help yourself," she said. "It's all under that affair there." She pointed to a frilled silk thing in the corner.

The disguises telephones take in modern houses amaze me. Lewis found his number and made a call.

"Pretty sickening, I call it," Boyd remarked with disgust as we went down in the lift.

"More than that," Lewis agreed. "Still, some

very interesting information there. We're getting on, I think. Will you find out whose 'phone number this is, Richard? And I'm going to call it a day."

He wrote a number on a slip of paper and handed it to Boyd.

CHAPTER NINE

LORD CHILTERN was unable to be in London constantly, even in this crisis in Catherine's affairs, and he requested me to keep in the closest touch with her and with Major Lewis, whom he directed me, as the family solicitor and friend of long standing, to help in every way possible.

I told him about my unfortunate conversation with Lewis about the settlement, and was considerably relieved when he assured me he thought I had taken the right action in the circumstances. While he was not anxious to have the Chiltern finances discussed by the public press, he agreed that Lewis should be put in possession of all possible details.

Indeed, as I thought the matter over after Lewis had left me the evening before, I found I had greater confidence in the large pleasant man with the slow rather inward smile. Resourcefulness and capability were somehow indelibly stamped on him. He is a gentleman and a cultivated man of the world. I was beginning to understand Boyd's extravagant devotion to him. Boyd, I learned, had been in his company during the war, and I gathered vaguely from his panegyric that without Lewis the Allies could hardly have won. But taking that with a large grain of salt, there was no doubt of his courage and his power to attract and hold the devotion of men. His success in the field of private inquiry was considerable, and though I never heard him refer to himself or anything he had ever done, I was quite ready to accept, but in a more sober and intelligent way, Boyd's estimate of the man.

When I joined them at Moreton Gardens Thursday morning they were upstairs in Scoville's room. Lewis had spread before him on the table a number of sheets that I saw were photographs of various things.

"Good morning, Braithwaite," he said. "Here's something to puzzle you a little more." He offered me a chair at the table and waved his hand at a section of the prints.

"These are the photographs of the finger-prints on the table and the revolver."

I waited anxiously for him to go on.

"And . . . well, whose would you say they are ?"

He looked at me with a quizzical expression that I found extremely annoying, in the circumstances.

"They are all positively identified," he continued slowly, "every one of them, as Nelson Scoville's."

"Then surely," I couldn't help but say, "it's clear enough that he shot himself ?"

Lewis shook his head, and Boyd groaned, half comically and half in dejection. "I wish it were as simple, Braithwaite," Lewis said. "But of course there are complications, aren't there ? This man was left-handed, to take the least. Everyone has verified that; I've even been to see his brother about it. But these prints are all of his right hand. Now a left-handed man isn't going to take his revolver in the wrong hand and inflict two mortal wounds on himself. Not one chance in a million.

"Furthermore, you have the two wounds, and again you have the absence of marks in the room; it all looks much too deliberate, some way, unless, of course, he planned it out very methodically. And then, finger-prints can easily be 'faked' — and have been, often. It wouldn't, for example, be impossible to fix them with his fingers on the butt of the revolver, when he was dead or dying. And these, although they're in the proper places, aren't quite clear and distinct. So, about all these pictures tell us is that Scoville had his right fingers on this revolver at some time."

He smiled pleasantly at my obvious reluctance to drop my theory.

"Surely," I urged, "if Mrs. Scoville knew he was left-handed, and if she *had* shot him, she would have put the thing in his left hand, not his right ? I mean, near it on the table ? Doesn't that clear her ?"

"That's reasonable, Braithwaite," he replied. "If there were nothing else, it might be enough. But say she did do it; there are two ways of explaining it. She forgot it in the stress of the moment; that's possible. Or, she did it deliberately to mislead, thinking that whoever came along would reason as you've done. Looking at her, I should say the latter is the more likely."

I looked at him in amazement. Then I had to admit that what he had said was quite true. Catherine certainly did not look the sort of person to lose her head in an emergency. Given the two alternatives, the latter was undoubtedly the more probable.

Boyd had said nothing during this conversation. He sat there smoking a cigarette, a heavy frown on his good-looking young face. Lewis got up and began thoughtfully pacing up and down in front of the window. I saw him look out with a smile.

"Our friend next door is vastly interested in this room still, Richard," he observed.

"Ah? The oologist et cetera? I put a man on to watch him, just for curiosity's sake. The watcher watched, eh? Mr. Maitland-Rice doesn't know about the unseen guest at every meal, or whatever it is. I hope he doesn't, anyway."

"Anything come of it?" Lewis asked absently.

"Nothing yet. We're going into his finances today. If there's anything queer about people it all comes out in their pass-books. Mind your pass-book, Braithwaite," he said solemnly. Then he added, "And that, by the way, is exactly what Scoville didn't do."

He picked up a folded sheet of paper that I had noticed on the table. "Look at this, Monk," he adjured, "and get the old skull working."

Lewis spread the paper out on the table. It was a statement of the dead man's affairs. He had outstanding debts owing to his tailor, his boot-maker, his haberdasher, his wine-merchant, and so on, of £3546. 9s.; to French dressmakers, £3324; and to money lenders of varying degrees of respect-ability, £12,268: a total of £16,138. 9s. He had in the bank £22. 7s.

"Moreover," Boyd said when we had finished looking at this curious record, "all these debts have been contracted in the last year. The tradesmen involved tell me that for the last five years his ex-penses have been greater than that, but there are no unpaid accounts beyond what we have before us. The brokers say he's borrowed the £12,268 within the year, on his prospects. Lord Scoville's will is settled, you see, the first of January. He hadn't borrowed from them, extensively anyway, until last spring, when he went to the continent."

Lewis nodded soberly. "And his income was £1000 a year." He was thinking intently.

"Good Heavens!" I cried suddenly. They looked at me in surprise. "The Muscovy Diamond is stolen! Can he have been living on that?"

Lewis shook his head. "No, it won't do, Braith-waite. I'm sure of that. Kracower, who is a very old and trusted friend of mine, knows more about diamonds than any other man in these parts. He says definitely that the Muscovy Diamond was safe last June at the end of the Hospital Bazaar. It was exhibited then for three days. It was examined when it came from the bank, and when it went back to the bank. Insurance people, very strict, and so on. Also, he is quite sure furthermore that it's not been on the market. He would have heard of it, he thinks, or at least rumors of it would be about in the fitting channels."

"That doesn't necessarily mean much, Monk," Boyd said. "It may be hid somewhere."

"I'm sure it is," Lewis returned, with a smile. "But the point is, Scoville wasn't living on it. Furthermore, though I'm no expert, I very much doubt if he could dispose of such a stone, in less than some years, at any rate."

"By the way," he continued thoughtfully, "why not see if young Davidson couldn't tell something about this. I'm going to ask him to come over. Got a suspicion he might be a little more willing to talk."

He gave Davidson a ring at once, and then started pacing the room again, it seemed to me almost absently examining every object as he passed it.

"What about that telephone number that seemed so popular with Miss Dean, Dickie?" he asked after some minutes' study. "Did you find it?"

"I did," Boyd answered promptly. "It sounds extremely unlikely to be of interest. The name is

James Henry Wills, the address No. 37, Shepherd's Bush Road. Interested ?"

"Rather. It's just a notion. Rather queer, don't you think, that the dainty Mimi should have an interest in Shepherd's Bush Road ? Still . . ."

He stopped abruptly and looked around the room. Then he walked over to the telephone. "Nothing here, eh ? Where's his memoranda pad ? Or where's the directory ?"

The latter loomed up enormous and red on the table, where we all saw it at once. Boyd seized it eagerly. We all leaned over the table, though I had no very clear idea of what we were looking for; and as Boyd took it, the book opened naturally, to reveal a thick sheet of notepaper. I think that again all of us recognized at the same time that it was Scoville's writing.

"Hello, hello !" Boyd said. He read aloud:

Mimi dearest —
I wanted to see you tonight. Why are you so capricious just now ? — we haven't time for play-acting. We've got to chuck it all, as we agreed. I don't think we'll mind it much, knowing we'll be together for always.

I've had a visit from our friend. You're right as ever. He suspects.

You're also right about C. She'll do anything now. I only hope she waits till we're ready for her. Then the joke will be on her.

WE LOOKED at one another in silence. Lewis had picked up the telephone directory and was running through it. Suddenly he whistled softly and laid it down open on the table. On the top margin towards the back was written in Scoville's hand, "James Henry Wills."

"Come, come!" Lewis said with a grin. "What with one thing and another, we're getting on! Now let me see that note."

He was still reading it over and over, with great interest and many frowns of perplexity, which I for one couldn't understand the reason of, when Flora announced Hartwell Davidson. A change had come over him since the day before. I couldn't say exactly what it was, but he seemed a little less confident, and much less belligerent. His fine straightforward eyes were anxious, and his hands in his jacket pockets moved incessantly.

He acknowledged our greeting shortly and sat down. Lewis offered him a cigarette from the box on the table, which he was in the act of taking, when Boyd said suddenly, "The Muscovy Diamond's gone, Davidson."

"Gone!" the man said. His surprise was certainly genuine. "You mean it's been stolen!"

"You know something about it, Davidson," Lewis stated calmly.

"Do you think I've got the damned thing? Is that why you got me here?"

"No. But you know something about it," Lewis

replied. "Tuesday night you went to the Hot
Pot Club to see Scoville. You were highly excited,
and you shouted 'Thief !' at him — or he at you.
I think it was the former. The diamond has gone.
We don't know of anything else missing. What's
the connection ? Scotland Yard has gone through
all likely places for it —"

"And some unlikely," Davidson broke in sardonically; "my rooms !" He glowered at Boyd,
who blew an elaborate smoke ring in the air.

"Very probably," Lewis went on. "What do
you know about it ?"

Davidson looked at him for a moment. Then
his face cleared up suddenly. "I'll tell you," he
said calmly.

"It was Lennert. He's from Hatton Garden,
and he's got a reputation of sorts for being helpful
in difficult matters, and that sort of thing. I've
known him since I was a boy. Well, he looked
me up Tuesday evening. It was just before dinner. He said he had something rather delicate to
tell me. Doing it as a friend, and so on. This is
what it was. That swine Scoville had 'approached'
him that afternoon to get him to take the Chiltern
diamond from him for £10,000. Lennert wanted
to know why so cheap, and Scoville said he needed
cash. Lennert said he'd think it over. He tried to
get in touch with me and couldn't. He thought
it over then until everything was closed up, and
then he got to Scoville and said he wouldn't handle

it. He found me at dinner and told me this. I started after Scoville and got hold of him at the club."

"Stout fellow !" Boyd said approvingly. "Then the row, eh ?"

"Just as I've told you. I left here about 12:30."

"The row was about the diamond ?" Lewis asked.

"Naturally. He said it was no go. He'd had to change his mind about the diamond because he couldn't get hold of it."

"Frank about it, wasn't he ?" Boyd observed.

I was astounded. "But, gentlemen," I cried, "that is absurd ! The diamond doesn't belong to him, in the first place, and in the second it's entailed ! It couldn't possibly . . ."

Major Lewis cut me short. "One thing more, Mr. Davidson," he said. "Why did Mr. Lennert go to you about the diamond ? Why not to Lord Chiltern ?"

"I've told you why. He's a friend of mine."

"But I'm afraid I don't quite understand what connection *you* have with the diamond ?"

Davidson flushed angrily. "I haven't any connection with the diamond. Lennert knows I'm a friend of Catherine Chiltern, and he knew I'd like to save her diamond for her if I could. If you think . . ."

The door opened suddenly. Catherine stepped

into the room, and looked from one of us to the other.

"What *is* this all about, Major Lewis ?" she said. "It's perfectly absurd to bring Mr. Davidson into this !" Her eyes sparkled with resentment, and her husky voice was vibrant with anger.

CHAPTER TEN

BOYD brought up a chair. "Sit down, Catherine," he interrupted. "I'm going to tell you what Mr. Davidson has told us. And then I'm going to ask you a few questions."

"Which you may or may not answer, Mrs. Scoville," Lewis added with a smile. There seemed to be something reassuring to Catherine in it, and she relaxed a little in her chair.

"Very well," she said, and listened quietly to the story Boyd repeated to her.

"I don't understand it at all," she said then. "I think there has been a mistake. My husband has not spoken to me at all about the diamond. And he knew it couldn't be sold, of course."

"But the diamond is gone, Catherine," Boyd exclaimed impatiently.

"Father told me. But I still believe there's a mistake. How can it be gone? And if it is you must find it. My husband may have done many things, but I do not believe that he was a thief." She spoke with a quiet dignity that impressed us all, except Boyd, who shrugged his shoulders and offered her a cigarette.

"Have you no notion when it disappeared?" he asked, quite as if she'd never spoken.

"None!" She ignored the implication.

"Will you let me give you some advice, Mrs. Scoville ?" Lewis said quietly. "If you don't wish to answer Mr. Boyd's questions, just say so; but if you do answer them, it's much the best plan to answer them truthfully."

We all stared at him. After all, one doesn't expect such language from a gentleman. Catherine flushed indignantly.

"I mean this," he continued calmly. "You are continuing to make two bad mistakes. You don't at all realize the danger of your position, and you badly underestimate the resourcefulness of the police. For instance, Mr. Boyd is aware that on Monday night there was a burglary, or an attempted burglary, at this house. We know from Hicks that the household burglar alarms, which ring in his room, were turned off by some one inside the house."

All the life had drained from Catherine's face. She sat dumbly, not attempting to deny or to explain.

"May we go into your sitting-room ?" he asked abruptly.

She nodded silently.

Across the hall Lewis made a rapid investigation of the room. In the corner to the right of the door, away from the windows, stood a beautiful Chinese Chippendale cupboard, one of those corner arrangements. Lewis opened the doors of the lower half and revealed a compact but stoutly built safe.

At the side of the room between the cupboard and the door he pointed to a small curious apparatus, concealed under the shelf of the book-cases.

"This is the latest thing in burglar alarms," he said, "the invisible ray.

"This" — he pointed to the small glassed aperture — "is a lamp glass that screens all visible rays, but lets through the infra-red or invisible ray. The ray is directed to a selenium bridge."

He crossed the room diagonally. By the door, about three feet from the floor, was another small device.

"This selenium cell, or bridge, is sensitive to light, including the infra-red ray. When an object crosses the light path, or in this case crosses the ray, a circuit is broken and a bell rings.

"On Monday night, after this alarm was set at 11 o'clock, some one crossed the path of the ray, broke the circuit, and rang the alarm. The alarm rings in two places: at the head of Mrs. Scoville's own bed"—he pointed to a tiny electric buzzer behind the night-table—" and at the offices of the Associated Night Watchers Ltd., at their branch in Fulham Road."

We returned to Scoville's room, where Catherine was sitting. She was apparently quite recovered from her agitation.

Lewis continued. "The alarm was given at about 1:30. Mrs. Scoville, you got up when the bell rang, took your revolver and crept to the door

of your sitting-room. You must tell us, please,
what you saw there."

He paused, but Catherine made no offer to
speak.

"Well," he went on steadily, "I can guess what
you saw. But whatever it was, you called the As-
sociation on the 'phone and told them that you had
yourself crossed the ray and broken the circuit
accidentally. But they had already sent two oper-
atives out. They arrived in three or four minutes.
You went downstairs to admit them. In doing so,
you unswitched the window and door alarms in the
cupboard in the hall, on your way down."

Catherine moved involuntarily; and Lewis
stopped. "Or they were already off," he said,
glancing casually at her. "In any case, you gave
the men who called a packet, telling them to give it
to the manager, and that you would call in the
morning for it. Which you did, Mrs. Scoville; in
the morning you called for it, and you took it to
Beacon's bank.

"So much is known, Mrs. Scoville. Don't you
see how futile it is for us to be going on in this
way?"

He stopped and lighted his pipe, which had gone
out during all this.

I was surprised at Catherine. She was quite herself again. "You're quite right in part of it," she
said, calmly enough, "but not in all. I did call up
the night-watching people, but what I told them

was quite true. I *had* crossed the ray by accident, and I called to tell them so. You see, I'd been away all summer and simply forgot about the thing. But when they came, I got the diamond and gave it to them, because . . . well, I wanted to get it out of the house."

"Why ?" Lewis asked.

She hesitated only a moment, then shrugged her shoulders. "I suppose I should have told you before, but it seemed so fanciful. Off and on the last week or two there's been a man with a barrel-organ at Chiltern. We'd never had one in the village before this year. He'd been around the Lodge too, a lot, and the other day I learned that he'd become friendly with some of the servants. Several days ago he disappeared, and we didn't see him there afterwards. I had the diamond in the country with me, you see, over the last week-end; I wore it at dinner for some of father's friends the night before. Well, I brought it up with me to take back to the bank. I was busy during the afternoon I got here, and hadn't time to go with it Monday; and when I got home, around six o'clock, I saw the man with a barrel-organ. He was playing on the corner. I was a little alarmed at seeing him. But it was too late to go to the bank. And so, after I gave the alarm I thought I might as well send the diamond to them in case anything did happen."

I thought she made it all quite clear.

Lewis and Boyd were looking steadily at her.

"In that case," Boyd said, "the thing must have been stolen some time ago, of course, and you unwittingly gave the watchmen the false one ?"

She seemed startled at that, but nodded silently. "I suppose so," she said rather weakly.

I noticed that in the short silence that followed Lewis and Boyd seemed to avoid looking at one another.

"Are you familiar with this telephone number ?" Lewis asked then. He held out a slip of paper to her.

She looked at it. "No. I don't know it. I suppose I may have called it some time. Has Inspector Boyd found that out too ?"

Her tone was pleasant enough to take the edge off the words but Boyd's voice had a shade of annoyance in it.

"I wish you'd realize, Catherine," he said, "that if we're going to keep you out of the dock — I might just as well speak plainly about it — we've got to find out who did this thing. Don't you see we're doing all we can to help you ? If you'd only . . . "

"I think Mrs. Scoville understands that," Lewis said. He hesitated a moment. Then he said, "Let's get at this other matter. I think there's something in it."

We all filed out. Davidson did not wait to speak to Catherine. Scarcely looking at her, he went down the stairs and out the door. The rest of us got into Boyd's car.   He drove up the Earl's Court Road towards Kensington High Street, none of us speaking.

Suddenly Boyd turned to Lewis and said, "What possible reason could the woman have for stealing her own diamond ?"

Lewis knocked out his pipe and put it in his pocket without answering.   I waited for him to speak, but he did not.   I wondered if he was thinking the same thing.

There was no further conversation.   After some minutes I ventured mildly to inquire our destination.

"Of course," Lewis answered.   "I'd forgot you weren't with us when we were talking about it. We're paying a social call on one James Henry Wills, at No. 37, Shepherd's Bush Road."

I suppose my surprise was very evident, for even Boyd, who seemed rather disgruntled with the events of the morning, chuckled at me.

"The point is this," Lewis explained.   "When Miss Dean telephoned to Scoville Wednesday morning, she asked, before she had realized that it was not Scoville speaking, if it was a certain number. In a jocular way.   I remembered the number; and I was rather interested in it, because although I didn't know what number it was, I knew it wasn't Scoville's.   Well, when we were in her rooms, I found it written in her directory, in very small figures at the bottom of a page.   So I developed a mild interest in it.   And after this morning, there's not much doubt that it has some meaning.   It's also written in Scoville's directory.   You remember I was looking for it when we found the note. Ergo, having looked up its owner — or reputed owner — we now visit Mr. Wills."

We had arrived somewhere near our destination by this time, and in a few minutes, with the aid of a constable and several small, very dirty and very acute urchins, we came to the address, in one of the more desolate side streets of the district.

I looked at the place with some curiosity.   It was a small dingy shop, with faded Cadbury cocoa posters leaning perilously against the dirty window. Flyspecked crêpe paper, whose yellow had faded years before, clung limply to the display boxes. Altogether a depressing place, and as far as I could see, of utterly no use to us.   Inside, Mr. Wills, we presumed, presided over a small stock of stale biscuits and tinned vegetables.   The bundles of firewood under the counter were the only items that looked at all recent, except perhaps the small case of a cheap brand of cigarettes.   Apparently the trade in them was brisk enough, which isn't surprising considering the neighborhood.

Mr. Wills was surprised, and eager to be of service.   Lewis bought a box of matches, explained that we were evidently, he was afraid, at the wrong address, and asked if he might use the telephone.   He was led to a tiny stuffy apartment, as it appeared from where we remained, in the rear of the shop.

Mr. Wills then returned. I drew him into a desultory conversation. He was anxious to talk, seeing, I suppose, few people, especially men, during the day. Trade was bad, I gathered. Unemployment struck people hard, in the district, and they had few enough coppers to spend for anything but bread and beer.

We continued talking when Lewis joined us. I noticed how deftly he swung the conversation around to the man's own situation.

Lor', no, he couldn't make a living out of the shop, even though he had only his wife and an afflicted daughter to do for. They rented the house, rents being still low about there, and let rooms and breakfast to four young fellows who worked for the railway. They each paid twelve shillings a week, so one got on, with what the shop brought in.

Lewis suggested gravely that the telephone was an extravagance in the circumstances. "Lor', no !" Mr. Wills accepted Lewis's pouch and filled his pipe. No, one of the things that kept his young men there was that they could use the 'phone. He also had a brisk trade from the neighboring flats. He charged three-ha'pence a call — Lewis handed him a sixpence — and, as he'd explained, he didn't have to pay the rent of the 'phone, only the calls. So he made a tidy sum.

Lewis remarked that he wished he didn't have to pay the rent of his. Mr. Wills rose to the bait.

He had the house from a retired grocer who had been there several years. He had a lease on the place, but had found the money to go to Canada. Wills had taken over the lease and found the telephone included.

Glancing casually at Lewis, I saw his eyes glisten at this; but to Mr. Wills there seemed nothing strange about it. No, he didn't know whom the house belonged to. He paid his rent quarter-day to the agents near the station. He'd been there five years next Easter.

Lewis turned the conversation to our own affairs. We were hunting for Mr. Yates and his wife, who lived around in the neighborhood. This caused Mr. Wills much painful thought. He obviously was distressed at not knowing them, and ticked off every one in the vicinity on his grimy hands. He concluded that they did not live on the Road; not, at least, under that name — a circumstance that seemed in no way unusual to him.

Lewis extracted several unmounted photographs from one of his baggy and enormous pockets. The way he did it made it seem a very normal proceeding, as if any of us, if he reached into his pockets, would customarily find photographs there. He put them on the counter in front of Wills; I could then see that they were photographs, as I expected, of Scoville and Miss Dean.

"These are the people," he said. The man studied them closely.

"No. I've never seen them," he said. Then suddenly he bent his head forward, picked up the picture of Mimi Dean, and held it at arm's length. Lewis's interest plainly quickened, and so did mine.

"Why, that . . . that's Mimi Dean, the actress, isn't it?" he said triumphantly. "I'd know her anywhere. Why, the paper had a contest last year to guess the picture actresses, and I won the third prize. A guinea and two tickets to her theatre."

He beamed at us with some pride. "One of my young men — he's a guard on the underground — has actresses' pictures all over his room." That seemed to be in partial explanation.

The other photograph he could not recognize, even after a prolonged study; and after a few minutes Lewis bought some packages of cigarettes, and we got out.

CHAPTER ELEVEN

BOYD was nowhere in sight.

"Probably got fed up with waiting," I remarked a little acidly.

"Oh no," Lewis said pleasantly. "He never gets fed up. We'll just wait a bit for him ourselves."

We did for ten minutes. Lewis then stepped back into the shop and returned immediately.

"I've left a message for him," he explained. "We can step along."

We walked, far too rapidly for my leisurely tastes, to the underground, came out at Tottenham Court Road, and walked around to Lewis's offices in Little Denmark Street. Lewis said nothing during our trip, and I eventually became a little uneasy, wondering if I should leave him. Not quite knowing the etiquette of the matter, I continued along.

Lewis's office I found to be extremely non-committal. His secretary, a quiet chap who had lost a leg in the war, was typing busily in a small room which we passed through. "Mr. Boyd 'phoned," he said. "He's coming here after a bit."

We sat down in a large room comfortably but very plainly furnished. After some minutes' thought Lewis said, "Now why, Braithwaite, should both Mimi and Scoville have been interested in the 'phone number of that wretched little place ?"

I couldn't offer any solution to the problem, and since long silences never seemed to bother him, I didn't feel called upon to say anything at all.

He was absently making squares and crossing them out when Boyd came in.

"Something jolly queer about that telephone," he said, helping himself to a cigarette. "I told the old bird he ought to report it."

Lewis looked up with more interest than he had shown for a long time. "Let's have it !" he said. "Also, what the devil happened to you ?"

"What indeed !" Boyd replied with a grin. "I've been dashing all over the beastly map. I was sitting quiet-like in my magnificent car, you see, waiting for a couple of asses to come out of a grocer's shop in Shepherd's Bush, when who should I see, his head hanging out of a taxi, trying to spot the house numbers, but . . . who would *you* say ?"

"Get on !" said Lewis.

"But Mr. Maitland-Rice, the oolithologist ! And at precisely the same moment he saw me; because he ducked back into the taxi and it shot off around the corner like a flash."

"What did you do ?" I asked.

"My dear Braithwaite, what *do* you think ? I followed him; yes, sir, I did. And Mr. Maitland-Rice went straight to the park, and got out, and hit out across the grass. What do you think of that ?   And there I left him to his nature studies."

"And then ?" Lewis prompted.   "The 'phone ?"

"Ah yes.   And then I went in a 'phone box and
rang you at Mr. Wills's, for ten solid minutes.
You didn't answer, you may remember. So I
dashed out.   The old boy was sitting just where
you'd left him, you'd just gone, and he said the
blasted 'phone hadn't rung !   Aha !"

He grinned at us in triumph.

Lewis's great hand came down on the desk
with a thunderous blow.   "By Jove, no more it
hadn't !" he exclaimed.   "Exactly right.   Dolt
that I am !"

"Yes, yes !" Boyd agreed.   "But what the . . .
I mean, why hadn't it ?"

"Well," Lewis said, "I had a peculiar feeling that
there was something wrong with that 'phone.   And
that was it.   There's no bell."

I stared at him uncomprehending.

"The thing's a blind," he went on vigorously.
"The 'phone is in Wills's name.   The number on
it is perfectly O. K.   You can call out, you see,
but you can't call in — at least not to Mr. Wills.
And there you are !   The real telephone is somewhere else.   When we find where, we're getting
along."

"Well, go on," Boyd said.   "What's the idea ?"
He was almost as puzzled, I imagine, as I was.

"The idea ?   Well, if you wanted a telephone
where people could call you, but one that you didn't

want traced to you, how would you go about it ? Obviously, you'd have it in the possession of a stupid little shop-keeper in Shepherd's Bush. Only, you give him an extension, and you take the 'phone with the bell. You take the main apparatus. He could call out, don't you see, if and when you didn't cut him off; and you'd explain to him, I dare say, that it was a one-way phone. Or most of his calls would be out, and he'd be too simple to realize he was never being called up himself. Or, more likely, he just about never did have an outside call. I'm speaking now, you realize, about Mr. Wills."

Boyd still looked a little unconvinced. "What about the Post Office ? They'd hardly stand such an arrangement."

"Don't be naïve. There are electricians. I could do it myself easily, and so could you. I dare say if you'll investigate you'll find there's somebody connected with this who pays rent for a telephone and an extension, the latter at present missing. Or you can buy an extension in the Caledonian Market. I offer these merely as suggestions."

"Then in that case," I ventured, "the other telephone, of which Wills's is the extension, can't be far away."

"Precisely," Lewis replied. "I suspect it to be next door, one way or the other. You might set some one to find out, Dickie."

"But even then," I went on, "I don't understand

why Mr. Maitland-Rice should have been out there."

"You don't ?" said Boyd. "Well, I'm damned if I do either." Lewis smiled at both of us and filled his pipe.

We separated at Boyd's office, Boyd to inquire at the Post Office about the telephone, I to attend a directors' meeting for an absent client. We arranged to meet there again after lunch. Until then I was completely in the dark as to their plans. I wanted rather badly to communicate with Lord Chiltern, but felt that after all I had nothing very reassuring to tell him about Catherine's situation or the situation in general, as far as that went. So I refrained.

And more than that, I was considerably dismayed at the apparent way in which Boyd avoided discussing that angle of the case in my presence. I found the whole matter, especially the trouble over Wills's telephone, decidedly perplexing. I'm afraid my whole-hearted attention to the affairs of Transylvania Ores Ltd. left a good deal to be desired.

Lewis was engaged when I came back. I confess I was a little annoyed at the thought of his having other matters than ours to occupy him. He was free, however, by Boyd's arrival.

"Inspector Boyd," he said cheerfully, motioning him to a chair, "will favor us with an intelligent report."

"Well, in the first place," Boyd replied with un-usual seriousness, "we can carry on as we are for the time being. I spoke to the Chief. He agrees with you, Monk, about Catherine. We haven't enough actual evidence to get a charge from a coroner's court. Thinks we'd better let it ride for a day or so. He's not so devilish enthusiastic. In fact I gathered from his manner and also from his words that he thinks things are moving about as fast as an ice-flow."

Lewis turned to me. "I think we should tell you," he said, "how we stand in regard to Mrs. Scoville."

I had felt this coming for some time, of course, and braced myself.

"There is a very strong circumstantial evidence against her. I won't go into it, it's pretty obvious. The evidence of Miss Dean, I think, is quite false, and can be shown to be so. But the fact that Mrs. Scoville is deliberately trying to mislead us, for some reason of her own, about that blessed dia-mond, makes our job very hard. Whom she's shielding I don't know. I thought Davidson at first. Perhaps he is the man. Or perhaps, of course, she's simply shielding herself."

He stopped and began to fill his pipe.

"It's simply a blooming mess, that's what it is," Boyd groaned. "It's getting pretty hopeless. I can hold off a couple of days. The Chief wanted to know if I didn't want some help from old Horsey

Harper. Yah! And yet I'd hate to arrest her, by Jove I would!"

"That's rot," Lewis said. "If she shot him she ought to be arrested, and you might as well do it as anybody. But let's get after Mr. Wills. 'The Abominable Mystery of the Bell-less Telephone.'"

CHAPTER TWELVE

ON OUR way out, Boyd detailed the history of the telephone, the 'abominable mystery' of which I for the life of me could not see. Still, I needn't say I was greatly interested. According to Boyd there was nothing irregular about it, at least on the face of things. It was in the name of Mr. Wills. The rental was paid by the estate agents. Nor was there anything unusual about them. But I noticed that Lewis was especially attentive when Boyd described the owner of the property.

He was a gentleman named N. V. Talbot, whose address — he appeared to have no settled location — was in care of the London and Provincial Bank in Shepherd's Bush. Apparently he was an eccentric. Most of his time was spent abroad. He had been in London during the spring and summer, and had left for the United States, in fact, only some two weeks before. Boyd had learned that among his other peculiarities he was a follower of the American Henry George — if I have the name right — and when in London frequently lived in one of his own rather cheap houses. He owned a number in various parts of the city, and had recently been living at No. 7, Oldfields Road, S. E.

"That's all very well," Lewis observed, when Boyd had finished. "But damn it, it doesn't explain why his tenants' 'phones haven't any bells. I wonder if he has a bell on his own 'phone. His name, by the way, is in the directory. Still, he's most probably perfectly genuine. I've noticed that most eccentric people are."

"In fact," Boyd said, "we'll probably find that one of Mr. Wills's young men has a flair for telephone engineering. I can't say I think much of your clue, Monk, or whatever you call 'em."

Lewis offered no defence of his theory, or his hopes, and I could see that he was not particularly sure of it himself. However, we continued on, and found Mr. Wills laboring diligently over a football competition. He was plainly a man of many interests.

Boyd explained that he was from Scotland Yard. The man was not greatly surprised, though somewhat worried until he learned what was wanted.

"I'm glad it's the telephone," he said eagerly. "I thought it was one of my young men. They get into trouble these days, what with early closing and the like. But I don't see what's wrong with the telephone. I had it gone over four years ago, and nobody ever bothered about it before today. There's you gentlemen, and about an hour ago there was another one asking about it. But there it is."

He followed us curiously into the back room. His feelings, I judged, were much like my own.

"So he came back," I heard Boyd say in an undertone.

Lewis nodded. "Pretty urgent, I fancy," he replied.

Lewis, it proved, was quite right. The bell apparatus was nowhere to be seen. The cord came through a properly lined aperture in the floor, and the instrument itself stood harmlessly on a table. We went down in the basement, and found dust and cobwebs for our pains. Upstairs we went through the grocer's apartments and those of his lodgers with no more success.

In the shop again Lewis put the man through a stiff pace, but his story remained precisely the same. One thing seemed conclusive. There was no other telephone on the grocer's premises. We left him, with that for a result, a little alarmed at the prospect of further visits, and I dare say exceedingly puzzled at the nature and purpose of ours.

We met a man from the telephone department as we stepped out, and without any unnecessary explanations Lewis told him what he wanted done. "I should judge," he said, "that the line comes from either of these houses." He pointed to the drab exteriors of Nos. 36 and 38. "Or," he added, "from the one across the back garden. There's no mews."

It seemed to me that Lewis was rather excited, although the only sign of it was his pipe, which he was puffing vigorously. It was actually burning.

"Go around and call on Mr. Talbot, Richard," he said, "our eccentric friend. That's his house in the rear. He isn't there, but he may have a caretaker. Ring the bell anyway, and wait till I come."

Rather then wait motionless I went with Boyd. We drove around to the other side of the block and stopped in front of another large match-box, almost an exact replica of No. 37. The house looked as much, or as little, occupied as any of the others. Cheap lace curtains hung in the windows, and the only difference I could see was the absence of unwashed milk bottles on the door step.

We rang the bell several times without response. Apparently we were not the only people looking for Mr. Talbot; we could hear the faint jingling of a telephone inside. Boyd rang again. We peered through the windows into the drab parlor. It had the usual ugly set of upholstered furniture and a floor lamp with a pathological red and yellow silk shade.

A voice suddenly accosted us from nowhere. "There ain't nobody home there," it said sharply. We looked around, then up. A shrewish person had thrust her head out of an upper window next door in reprimand. "Mr. Talbot ain't been home for more'n a week," she added more amiably, when we turned around.

Boyd raised his hat politely. "Thanks very much," he said. We went down to the car.

Lewis joined us almost at once. "No one at home," Boyd reported. "Been away for a week or so."

"Yes.   What about the 'phone ?"

"How do I know ?   I said there was nobody . . ." Boyd stopped abruptly and looked at me with a sheepish grin. "What a dizzy ass I am ! We heard it ring, of course.   Was that you ?"

Lewis nodded with a smile. "Yes, my friends. It was.   It was me ringing Mr. Wills's number. It's Mr. Talbot's 'phone we want, it's Mr. Talbot's house we've got to get into; and I've a suspicion that we're going to be rather interested in Mr. Talbot himself."

While Boyd went to Scotland Yard for a search warrant, Lewis and I returned to his office. "That's the handicap of working with the police," Lewis said with a grin. "You and I, Braithwaite, could climb in through the kitchen windows if we were alone.   We'll ring up the agent, Richard, while we're waiting for you."

"I suppose the diamond is as good a pretext as any," Boyd said, and departed.

As we came into Lewis's office, his secretary said, "Tate is waiting for you, sir."

"What's the matter with him ?" Lewis asked. "I didn't expect him until eight."

Tate, a rather ordinary looking person in ordinary clothes —this characteristic, I learned later, was one of the reasons of his success — was smoking very disconsolately in Lewis's room. "I lost her, sir," he said sheepishly. "And what's more, that's twice I've done it."

"Twice ?" Lewis said.

"Yes, sir; twice." The man seemed quite willing to censure himself roundly. "Yesterday I didn't mention it in my report, because it looked all right. It was perfectly natural, I mean."

"Never mind that," Lewis said. "Let's have it now."

"Well, sir, when you 'phoned, yesterday, I started right out like you said. I know Miss Dean by sight, so it wasn't any job starting. She got in her blue Rolls Royce and drove along Park Lane towards Piccadilly. She turned up Knightsbridge and stopped at one of those big drapers'. I followed her in, and it was easy to spot her, because she had a grey fur coat on and there aren't so many about this early.

"She got some stockings and I followed her along to the perfumery. Then she took a small lift. I didn't like to crowd in and step on her feet, so I went up the stairway. She wasn't on the first floor, and I couldn't find her on the second. I got all mixed up in the baby section. When I got straight she was too far off for me to find, I figured, wherever she'd got to. So I beat it back to the street and kept an eye on her car. In about half an hour out she comes with another lady. Then I followed them all day like I said in my sheet."

Lewis nodded. "That's not so bad," he said. "It would be pretty hard to keep at a woman's elbow in a departmental shop. What about to-day ?"

The man squirmed. He was obviously not proud of his recent work.

"Well, sir, I guess she had me badly today. I was at her flat early. The doorman said she didn't get up till noon, but I stayed around. I'd give him a pound to keep me posted. She came out just before one and trips off towards Oxford Street. I got over to the doorman quick: he said she told him she was doing a little shopping and she'd be back in half an hour, but if anybody came, to say she wouldn't be back until evening."

"Go on."

"I got in the tube just behind her and we did her shopping. She went to a Cook's place on the Strand and got back to Holborn. I began to think maybe she'd seen me. She's pretty smart. So I kept quite a ways behind. She went into the Holborn underground. It was crowded, so I followed her easier and got into the lift just as it went down. But I didn't see her on the platform, and I've not seen her since. I went to the house and waited, but she didn't turn up, so I came here. She sure is neat," he added, ruefully.

"At Holborn, was it ?" Lewis said.

The man nodded.

"Well, my lad, some time you go to the Holborn

Station and figure out what happened. Just now you'd better get back to Park Lane. If she doesn't come in by eight o'clock go home and go to bed."

Tate retired in dejection. Lewis smiled. "That's pretty hard for him to take," he said. "He's a good man for that sort of thing, and she did him nicely."

"Do you know what happened to her?" I asked.

"Pretty well, I think. In the Holborn Station you go into the lifts which look directly out on Kingsway. Pretty often, when you go in, you'll find the outside gates aren't closed yet. I think we'll find that's about what Mimi had noticed too. She knew Tate was following her, so she walked into the lift, knowing he'd wait until a good many people got in between them, and then she calmly walked out into Kingsway before the collector said 'Mind the gates, please.' I suppose she got a taxi. Might just as well see about that, by the way."

He put in a call to the Kingsway taxi rank and asked if any one had picked up a fare outside the station around one o'clock. He described the girl and waited.

"Thanks," I heard him say. "Have him ring Soho 6541." He hung up. "The head man remembers her. She took No. 3 off the rank. We may hear from him later."

He sat thinking for a moment. Finally he

reached for the telephone again and I was surprised to hear him ring Catherine's number. I
waited anxiously to hear what he would say to her.
His face gradually lost its expression of amused
geniality and became a mask on which I could
read nothing. Dismay gripped me as I watched
him. Without speaking he hung up the 'phone.

"Mrs. Scoville is out," he said abruptly, a frown
on his forehead.

"Out !" I exclaimed. "But she promised not
to leave the house !"

"Quite," he replied, and called through to Scotland Yard.

When Boyd came in shortly he was also worried.
"Where in hell did she go ? The beastly ass of a
constable says he saw her after luncheon. She
said she was going to lie down and nobody has seen
her since."

Lewis shrugged his heavy shoulders expressively.
"Never mind," he said. "Let her be. We'll find
her later. Now for Mr. Talbot."

The estate agent's timid assistant was in great
distress about the search. Their client's wife was
around; but he didn't know where, and he eventually supposed the proper person to serve such a
paper was probably the firm. As the manager
was out, he supposed the proper person was even
himself. He fiddled about saying, "Dear me, he
hoped nothing was wrong" until I thought Boyd
would strike him. I had not known that getting

into someone else's house involved so much running aimlessly about.

Once in, as a matter of fact, we found little
enough to reward this labor. The parlor offered
nothing we had not guessed from the view through
the curtains. The dining-room offered nothing
one couldn't guess from seeing the parlor. It was
the same throughout. Clean enough, but hopelessly drab, ugly, and middle-class. Several copies
of the *Daily Mail* were found, neatly folded up,
together with a Bible and Rider Haggard's *She*.
And upstairs it was the same story, except for one
small room.

We were just entering it when we stopped short
on the threshold: a telephone inside jingled ear-
splittingly. Lewis quickly motioned to the agent,
who took down the receiver and spoke. Lewis
interrupted him after he had said "Hello, are you
there" a half-dozen times, and took the instrument
himself. As he did so, we could all hear clearly
the click of the receiver at the other end. Whoever it was had replaced it quietly on the hook
without speaking a word.

Lewis signalled the operator. "This is Inspector Boyd of Scotland Yard," he said. "Please trace
the call that just came through here."

We waited almost breathlessly — or perhaps I
should say that I, at any rate, did. "Thank you,"
Lewis said, at last. He replaced the ear-piece,
hesitated a second, and then said, "It came from

Kensington 0345." My relief must have been evident, for he looked at me with a half-smile as he took up the directory. Over his shoulder I saw him turn to the S's and then to the M's.

"It's our friend the bird-man," he said with a chuckle. We all laughed, myself most of all, I suppose. I don't know exactly who I was afraid it might be.

Lewis and Boyd began a search of the room. It had the appearance of an office. There were two telephones, one, I gathered, being in Mr. Talbot's name, and the other, over which Lewis had just spoken, the one registered in the name of Wills. There was a desk, a typewriter, and a couple of chairs. Nothing else.

Lewis bent over the desk. "There's been something here till recently," he remarked, pointing to an oblong space quite free from dust.

"And not gone very long," Boyd added, rubbing his finger lightly over the polished surface.

They then went through the desk drawers, but without any success. Whoever had moved the object on the desk had cleared out the place thoroughly. There wasn't so much as a postage stamp. As we were going out, Lewis took a piece of paper from his note-book, put it in the typewriter; he typed a few lines on it, folded it up and placed it back in the book.

It was getting dark as we made our way downstairs and out the front door. Just as we closed it we heard the telephone ring clamorously. Lewis said something to Boyd in a tone too low for me to hear.

The woman next door was watching us with unconcealed curiosity. "I hope nothing's wrong, sir," she said pointedly.

"Nothing at all," Lewis said.

"I told Mrs. Talbot you was looking for her," she continued.

"*Did* you," said Lewis. "She's been here?"

"Oh, yes, sir. Came about half an hour after these gentleman had left. About three o'clock, it would be." She blossomed under the gentlemen's interest.

Lewis drew out his photographs.

"I have a picture of the Talbots with me — or I think it's they," he said agreeably, and handed them to her. "Right?" ,

But she looked back at him with visible suspicion.

"No, sir! That ain't the Talbots." She examined them again. "Why, that's Mimi Dean! That ain't Mrs. Talbot."

Then she chuckled with excitement.

"I'll bet you're one of those advertising men you read about. But Lord bless you, Mrs. Talbot is taller and bigger than Mimi Dean. And what's more, she's got brown hair. Mimi Dean's is yellow. I've seen her. And I've seen Mrs. Talbot too. Brown hair, she has."

We got into Boyd's car without a word. Each knew what was in the others' minds.

Catherine has brown hair and is taller than Mimi Dean.

CHAPTER THIRTEEN

BOYD had been talking to Catherine some time before I got to the house the next morning. With what success was evident from his manner.

"That damn girl!" he said with exasperation. "Anybody would think she wanted to hang for the murder of that awful person. She's beyond me. She refuses, in spite of everything, to say where she was, what she was doing, or who she was with yesterday."

Lewis shook his head. "Well, we've got to make a go at it in spite of her. Did you see Maitland-Rice ?"

"Last night," Boyd said. "I waited for the blighter until 11:30. He came home in a frightful whack. I thought he was drunk at first, but he wasn't. I had to let him have a couple of stiff ones before I could get much out of him."

"Where had he been ?"

"Sitting up with the little feathered friends, I fancy. He said he'd been nowhere, and stuck to it."

"What about the 'phone calls ?"

"Denied it flatly. Hadn't been home all afternoon. The butler said so far as his knowledge went he had been out. He was cleaning silver, or whatever butlers do, in the basement kitchen."

"And this morning ?" Lewis asked patiently.

"Declined any information. Just gone to see a man about a dog. Denied flatly being in Shepherd's Bush."

"What about Scoville ?"

"Knew Scoville a little. They belonged to a club. Doesn't know him very well."

"Miss Dean ?"

"Knows her from her pictures. That's all I got out of him. In general, in other words, I've had rotten luck. — Now what to do ?"

Lewis thought about it. At least he filled his pipe and lighted it with even more than his customary leisureliness.

"Well," he said, stopping to tamp his tobacco down with the side of the match-box — a performance that I always expect to see end in a blaze of flame — "let's see what we've got.

"That it's murder, we're pretty well agreed. Except Braithwaite — I suppose ?" he added, smiling at me.

"Catherine Chiltern," I said, "is not capable of a crime of that nature; or of any other. I'm sure of that, at any rate."

"I wish she'd be as frank about it as you are, Braithwaite," Boyd said with a groan.

Lewis continued his summary with a smile. "In any case, murder seems to have been done, doesn't it? (a) A left-handed man wouldn't shoot himself holding the revolver in his right hand. It's

decidedly an anomaly. [Boyd: "Hear, hear!"]
(*b*) The two wounds, either of which was mortal,
make suicide virtually impossible. (*c*) While one
wound shows burning and powder-stain, the other
has no trace of either. No, it seems impossible to
get away from; it's simply a case of murder, and
apparently deliberately planned murder. Barring,
of course, some new evidence that we can't — or
I can't — now foresee.

"Now, the chief fact we have to go on, unfortunately, is that Mrs. Scoville had every possible reason for killing the man, and every possible
opportunity, and has not yet chosen to be frank
with us about the matter. That's a very bad combination of points.

"As for Miss Dean's evidence. She heard Mrs.
Scoville, it would seem, in the room on the night,
and at approximately the time, of the murder.
She heard a quarrel, and two shots. That's all very
telling evidence, of course; but for several reasons
we can go into later, I find myself tending not to
take it very seriously."

"Do you mean . . ." I began in surprise.

"I don't believe a word of it. Now, against
these things, we have Flora's statement, and Mrs.
Scoville's. I don't believe a word of them either.

"In fact, we only know two things about Mrs.
Scoville: the first, that somehow we don't think
she did it, and the second that Boyd, as an official
of public justice, has a good circumstantial case

against her, but not good enough.   It's not enough
to convince him, or us, and it's by no means enough
to get a verdict.   Ugly husband, beautiful woman,
plainest case of mistreatment, — no, your circumstantial evidence won't do.

"Now we have certain other people.   Hicks and
Flora haven't told us the truth yet.   I'm convinced of that.   Davidson we can pass over for the
time.   As for Mr. Maitland-Rice, and his strange
interest in the Shepherd's Bush mansion of Mr. and
Mrs. Talbot, I find that of the greatest interest."

Here Major Lewis stopped and sank into a
study prefaced by the interminable re-lighting of
his pipe, which appeared to be lasting indefinitely
until sardonically interrupted by Boyd.

"Now I consider that," he began, "a very keen,
lucid, and pregnant anal —"

"Shut up," said Lewis, recalling himself.   "Listen.   We are now going to see Miss Dean again.
I think we might find out something about Mr.
Maitland-Rice from her.   If not, maybe we'll
find out a little more about Mimi Dean."

As I look back on those words, I shudder to think
how unconsciously prophetic they were.   Some
people believe it is a blessed dispensation that hides
the future from each of us, as we should never be
strong enough to face it.   It surely is equally a
blessing that we can't know what is happening to
other people while our lives move placidly on.

Life would otherwise be an incessant nightmare, I'm afraid.

In Park Lane we saw Miss Dean's trim maid hurrying into the servants' entrance.

"She's late," Lewis observed. "Which is clear as well from her manner as from my watch. Mimi will probably be waiting for her breakfast. Tate, by the way, says she was in early last night. She was just arriving when he got here yesterday, after his sad experience at the Holborn Station," he continued, turning to me. "She'd been to tea with a crowd of youngsters and had a gay time. Tate was extremely annoyed to think she'd given him the slip just to have a tea-party. He felt the least she could have done was rob the Bank of England. She went to the theatre, the Hot Pot Club, and came home alone a little before one o'clock. Tate watched till two and went home."

"I hope she didn't go out again after that," Boyd murmured. "Night air being notoriously bad for young gels."

When we came to Miss Dean's door the maid was just going in. Boyd grinned pleasantly at her.

"I'll catch it," she said with a grimace.

"Don't worry. We're coming along, so you won't. Tell Miss Dean we're sorry and all that, but we must see her just as soon as it can be proper."

She looked at us dubiously, but admitted us into the drawing-room, and drew the heavy silk curtains to let in the pale November light. I hadn't realized how far gone the leaves were until then, as I glanced out across the Park. I was about to comment on it to Lewis, when a terrible shriek came out of the inner rooms, appalling through the morning quiet.

We stood rooted to our places an instant, before we sprang through the door to Mimi's bedroom. It was empty. The maid, her eyes wide with terror, stood white and speechless in a doorway, pointing past her. Lewis was beside her first; and by the sudden unconscious movement of revulsion he made, I knew that something dreadful awaited us.

Boyd drew the girl aside and pushed her into a chair, and we joined Lewis in the doorway.

On the soft rose and cream tiles of the bathroom floor lay Mimi Dean. Her honey-colored head hung backwards over the sunken bath (it's strange that even at such a moment I couldn't help making a mental note that it was not a tub but a pool); her lovely face was hideously swollen and distorted. Her hands clutched the air like claws, and her silken-clad body was grotesquely convulsed.

We stood there an instant literally frozen with horror. "Good God, what an end!" Boyd said in a whisper as he and Lewis knelt by her side.

"She's been dead hours," Lewis said gravely. "Call the doctor, will you, while I look about."

We closed the door on that terrible sight.

"Look after the girl, Braithwaite, please," Lewis

said. I couldn't think of anything but water. I got that, but she didn't want it. So I left her in the drawing-room and went back to see what was being done. Lewis was standing by the woman's bed. He picked up a letter that was lying under the edge of the rumpled silk eiderdown and glanced through it. A grim smile appeared on his face and gradually vanished. He glanced quickly about the room and knelt down by the bed. He rose with a square dispatch case in his hand. Without opening it he put it on a chair in the corner of the room near the window and laid his overcoat across it.

Coming back, his eye met mine. I don't think he knew I'd been standing there in the doorway. He smiled faintly at me, not in the least embarrassed, nor did he offer any explanation of his curious conduct.

"Look at this, Richard," he said, as that young man came back into the room. There was an air of disarray about the bed in general, and I stepped over by it to see more clearly what he was pointing at. A glass of water had been overturned on the night-table, and on the floor was the box of chocolates that we had noticed on our earlier visit. The few remaining pieces were scattered over the rug as if they had suddenly been thrown down with violence.

"This is pretty clear, I'm afraid," Lewis said. "She was in bed, reading this letter probably, at any rate eating these things. Tate says she came here without supper. She felt ill suddenly, and rushed to the bathroom. She was terribly sick, and probably couldn't get to the 'phone. I think you'll find that these chocolates aren't as innocent as they look."

"Do you mean the girl was poisoned by them ?" I almost screamed.

"Surely," he answered quietly.

It amazes me, how calmly some people can take the hideous realities of violent death.

"But good God, man !" Boyd said, with a grin. "I ate one of the things myself !"

"Lucky fellow !" Lewis replied tersely. "You chose well. Try one of these ?"

Boyd promptly declined, and as he did so the police surgeon came in with a troop of constables and pressmen, and he led them off to the bath. Lewis went into the kitchen, where the maid, white and pitifully frightened, was waiting helplessly. I followed him.

"Tell me just what happened," he said gently.

At first she couldn't speak, but his kindliness seemed to reassure her and she broke into voluble lamentations.

"Oh the poor lady ! I came in just like I was, you saw me. I thought she was up, because the lights were on in her bedroom, and I thought she just hadn't pulled the curtains. I turned them off and pulled the curtains and came in here to take

off my things. Then it seemed funny I didn't
hear her. She's usually singing in the mornings.
I got a little worried, so I tapped on the door and
called. But she didn't answer, so I pushed it open.
And there she lay, all terrible, the poor thing !"

"It was you who turned the lights off, then ?"

"Oh yes, sir." The girl was frightened again.
"Shouldn't I have ?"

"Yes, indeed. Quite right. You didn't
straighten anything up ? Pick any thing up off the
floor ?"

"No, sir, — Oh yes: there was a letter I put on
the dressing table."

Lewis left abruptly. Just what his interest in
the dead girl's correspondence was, I couldn't
fathom. In the circumstances it seemed a little
indelicate to me. And why he was withholding
evidence from the police — it was obviously what
he was doing — I couldn't see either. But I was
so badly shaken by all this that I didn't ask him
about it.

The doctor came out with Boyd.

"Arsenic poisoning," he said curtly. Boyd
handed him the box of chocolates. He broke one
of them and touched it gingerly to the tip of his
tongue. "That's it. Probably enough in one of
these to kill her. I'll tell you how much after the
autopsy. I should say she's been dead about nine
hours, if that's any use to you. But this stuff's

tricky. It could kill her possibly in ten minutes, or it could take a couple of hours. Beastly, rotten stuff. Very painful."

He returned the chocolates to Boyd, and giving some directions to one of the constables, went about his business in what seemed to me a remarkably cheery fashion.

Boyd, for some reason, had arranged for the general business of the police to be concluded with more dispatch than usual. The girl's body was removed to the mortuary and the chocolates sealed and sent off to Scotland Yard. We were alone again in a quarter of an hour; it scarcely seemed possible that so much had happened in so short a time. I noticed that no one paid any attention to the case under Lewis's overcoat on the chair, and wondered what he was going to do. He came out to us, when the men had gone.

"Molly," he said, "I want you to go through Miss Dean's things, very carefully, and tell me if anything is missing. Any thing at all — do you understand? I know it's rather hard to tell, but it'll help us to find out who did this."

The maid, a pert, courageous little thing, had pulled herself together, and her answer surprised us. "Oh, but I know who did it!" she said savagely. "It's that gentleman that's been ringing her on the 'phone every few minutes, and coming around to the theatre. He was there last night, trying to get in, and I caught him!"

"Who is he ?" said Boyd quickly.

"I don't know his name; he never gives it, and she knew him anyway. She always laughed when he called up. She'd never speak to him, though."

"What's he like ?"

"Well, he's about middle size. And he's about forty. Quiet, and he looked pretty worried. He's not dark or light, medium, if you know what I mean. Oh, I don't know ! I can't seem to be able to tell what he's like. But I'd know him. Or his voice, I could tell that too."

"Over the telephone ?" Lewis asked.

"Oh yes, of course I could."

Lewis went to the telephone in the drawing-room and rang a number. I couldn't hear what name he asked for. He signed to Molly and held the receiver to her ear. We heard her cry of recognition; and Lewis hung the receiver up at once.

He came back to where we were. "I should have Mr. Maitland-Rice detained, Richard," he said gravely. "Yet I wonder . . ." Then, after a moment's thought, he added vigorously, "Of course ! Better get hold of him, Richard, and right away !"

"Maitland-Rice ?" Boyd inquired, a little blankly.

"Yes, you blinking ass, Maitland-Rice." The maid was going through the wardrobes and was out of hearing, but he lowered his voice. "That girl had taken enough arsenic, if I'm not mistaken, to kill a horse. Maitland-Rice is an ornithologist, and he has tons of the stuff to preserve his damned birds with."

"But the motive!" I said. I felt extremely confused by all this, but things were being done much too precipitately for the peace of my "legal mind." I know that so eminent a person as Sir Beauvais Biron has recently pronounced that the police should act on suspicion, the magistrates on proof; but I disliked the idea of a person of Maitland-Rice's social standing being dragged to the police station because he was an ornithologist.

"Motive and to spare," Lewis said shortly. He handed Boyd the two letters he had picked up, one from the bed and one that Molly had put on the dressing table.

Boyd glanced hastily through them. "Dear me!" he said. "So that's what it was all about, eh, you old devil?"

He glanced admiringly at Lewis. "You sly old dog, you knew it all the time, eh?"

He looked back at the letters. "Giving him a bad time, wasn't she? In fact, things were so bad that Mr. Maitland-Rice was willing to pay £5000 . . . hm! hm! . . . which — let me see — which 'would practically beggar him' . . . if she will return his letters. You're right, Monk."

He went to the drawing-room and closed the door. I couldn't hear what he said to Scotland Yard.

CHAPTER FOURTEEN

LEWIS turned his attention to his pipe, and to the girl, who had finished looking through Miss Dean's effects.

"There's nothing missing, sir," she said. "Except — but it's not really missing, it's been gone several days, to be mended."

"What is *it* ?" Lewis asked.

"Her squirrel coat. She wore it Tuesday morning and caught the pocket on something, so she left it to be mended."

"Ah well," Lewis said absently. "I suppose she has a good many others."

"Only this, sir, that she wore home." The maid pointed to a grey fur coat in the wardrobe. "It's only imitation. She was going to give it to me when she got her other one back."

"Nice of her," Lewis remarked.

"Yes, sir. She was going out to lunch, and she was wearing a powder-blue dress and hat, so she had to have a grey coat. And when the one she had tore, she just got this. She'd promised to buy me a fur coat this winter anyway, so she said I could have this when she didn't need it any longer."

The girl was naturally insistent on that point, and Lewis smiled his complete consent as far as the matter concerned him.

"I'll tell the police about it," he said. "There's nothing else missing?"

"Nothing, sir."

"And nothing there she doesn't usually wear? I mean, nothing you don't recognize as hers?"

"Oh, no, sir." She was puzzled by that.

"That's all, then, Molly. You'll be wanted for the inquest, and if I were you I'd talk about this as little as possible."

She nodded. "Lady's maids have to be discreet, sir." She departed with that parting shot, at which Lewis smiled a little grimly.

Boyd returned. "That's done," he said. "They're keeping him at his house until I get out."

"Look here, Richard," Lewis said abruptly. "I held these out, because I didn't want the reporters even to sniff them." He pulled out the dispatch case. "Let's have a look at them."

He put the case on a table and opened it. It was full of letters, tied in neat bundles and docketed. Some of them looked years old, in that indefinable way that paper has of growing old. They looked through several packets, their faces registering, I thought, surprise, comprehension, and disgust.

After a while Boyd, with a short exclamation, put his bundle back in the case. "Damned if I can stomach any more right now, Monk," he said.

"These," Lewis replied, "are apparently what Mr. Maitland-Rice was willing to pay his £5000 for."

"He *is* the man, is he ? Did he know the fair Mimi too ? Better than most ?"

"Well enough. And she's been bleeding him ever since. It's all too clear. Look here: this is a set of demands. Folded. They've probably been returned. I wonder if somebody had guts enough to refuse ? Or perhaps the victim changed his address permanently. These demand payment of 'the usual £1000.' Phew !"

I must admit I was only half listening to them; my mind kept returning to the poor girl and her awful death. I gathered, however, that these were intimate papers that had been illegally used, and said so.

"You should be in our business, Braithwaite," Boyd replied gravely. "You're absolutely right. We call it blackmail. There's a great deal of inflammable matter here, and the pretty Miss Dean — peace to her ! — has been making use of it for some years."

"About five, to be exact," Lewis added coolly. "And she's made a pretty thing of it, I should think. There's one chap here I knew. He came around to me some months ago. Hinted about blackmail, letters, his wife's family, and so on. He got cold feet when I told him it was a coward's business, that he ought to tell them to go to hell. I didn't hear any more about it; and here it is."

"Did he know who was doing it ?" Boyd asked.

"I think not. What'll we do with these ?"

"You can burn them, or give them back to the owners."

"Better that. Then they'll know they're through, and not always afraid hell will break loose when they're least expecting it. But you're the official. Take this thing, and for God's sake don't lose it.

"Now I'm going around to Mimi's theatre," Lewis continued, "and then to the Hot Pot Club. Oh, by the way, I saw Kracower last night. He says the Muscovy Diamond is positively not on the market. He's pretty sure nobody else — that means the regular irregulars — has it. The imitation was made by Müller in Amsterdam, for an English gentleman who furnished him all the measurements, weight, etc., and paid him £110 for it. That was last year. Müller, of course, was quite above-board about it. He made a trip here to see it. It was wanted, so he was told, for exhibition purposes."

"Where the devil is it, then ?" demanded Boyd.

"Ah, that's what we must find out. See you later. Are you coming with me, Braithwaite ?"

I went with him. First to lunch — I was surprised to find that I was hungry, after the dreadful shock I had received in the poor girl's place — and then to the Century Theatre in Shaftesbury Avenue. The manager was almost beside himself. She had been the backbone of a thin and decrepit comedy that had played to full houses for several months and showed no signs of losing favor with her public. He was closing at once.

Beside that, he was genuinely shocked. "Pretty little thing, hard as nails," he said. He cocked a fishy eye at Lewis. "Scoville murdered too; how about that? Where's the connection, Major Lewis?"

Lewis assured him it wouldn't be long before the problem was solved, and got us admitted to the star's dressing-room. My only acquaintance with such places, of course, is through the cinema, which I occasionally attend. I discovered this one to be quite different. Or perhaps in America they really are as they picture them. Mimi Dean's room was a business-like place. Her various clothes were neatly hung up. There were no luxurious divans, or fountains, or tropical birds, or exotic plants. Lewis went through the paraphernalia with a practised hand. I could tell he was not being very successful, however. But he went through everything, — dresses, costumes of all sorts, wigs, even the table full of cosmetics.

On our way out he questioned the doorman. He admitted that on the evening before he had let in a gentleman — for a consideration — but Miss Dean's maid had put him out without ceremony. He didn't know the gentleman — had never seen him before.

At the Hot Pot Club our procedure was much the same; and so were the results. If the Chiltern diamond was hidden at either place, it would never be found, I thought, by human effort.   Lewis left nothing unsearched.

"No go," he said at last.   "We may as well go out to Kensington.   Here's the station."   I was glad he had left his absurd car at home; I found the tube much more comfortable.

I must admit I was still a little distrait from the morning's experience; I couldn't get the picture of that terrible bathroom out of my mind.   I suggested a little timidly to Lewis that we stop at my rooms in Hans Crescent, on our way out, for half an hour and have a drink.   He agreed very readily.

It was a new experience to me, having an enquiry agent in my own digs.   Not, of course, that there was anything there that I wished to hide; but I could not but be aware that his genial indifferent eyes saw everything.   We had a glass or two of some excellent whisky a client had sent me last Christmas — I keep it for special occasions — and sat there a few minutes, talking about Scoville and the Chilterns.

"What I can't make out," Lewis said after some desultory talk, "is how she could bring herself to marry him.   Never saw such a face on a man.   He seems to me to have been . . ."

"But he really wasn't, you know," I broke in. I was eager to defend Catherine, I suppose.   "At least, not when she married him.   On the contrary, he was a fine-looking man.   A little . . . er

. . . florid, perhaps, but quite all right. The Chilterns needed money, I know, but none of us had the remotest suspicion it could turn out so badly."

"Still, he must have been pretty much the . . . florid — as you say — man-about-town sort," Lewis continued.

"Not exactly," I said. "He was a sportsman of sorts. He was quite a handsome chap. As a matter of fact, I think I've got a picture of him then."

I had a photograph of him that appeared in *Country Life* just before their marriage. They were shooting in Scotland at Lord Cairn's place. It was a good picture of him, and Catherine was very lovely in her tweeds sitting on a boulder with the heather all about. I got the magazine with difficulty — it was in the bottom of my book-case — and found the photograph.

Lewis studied it with interest while I poured us another drink. And then he uttered a startled exclamation.

"What's wrong ?" I asked.

"Good Lord, Braithwaite !" he said, and handed the picture over to me. "What's he doing ?"

"Why," I said, "he's shooting, naturally; he's aiming with his gun."

"But not naturally !" he replied. "Don't you see ? He's shooting — with his right hand !"

I don't suppose it was more than ten minutes later that we found ourselves in Moreton Gardens again. Lewis was silently absorbed in gazing about the room, walking to the window, standing in front of the desk; acting, indeed, very curiously.

"Ask Mrs. Scoville to come in here, will you, Braithwaite?" he said suddenly. I was rather startled, but his expression hardly invited inquiries.

Catherine was reading in her room. She went along without comment, and was altogether, I thought, a little less tense than before.

"Will you sit down, please," Lewis said. "I'm at a point where you *must* be perfectly frank with me."

"Very well, Major Lewis," she said calmly.

"Did you shoot your husband?"

"No. I did not."

He smiled faintly. "Who is Mr. Talbot?"

She looked puzzled. "Do you mean Sir George Talbot?"

"No. Mr. N. V. Talbot."

"I'm sorry I can't help you, then. Sir George is the only one I know."

"Nor a Mrs. Talbot?"

"No. Other than Lady Talbot."

"Where were you yesterday afternoon?"

"I was at a French pastry shop in Earl's Court Road having tea." She spoke a little defiantly.

"With Mr. Davidson?" he asked.

"Oh, yes. How did you know?"

"It was just a guess, Mrs. Scoville," he replied absently. There was a shade of excitement in his manner and I looked at him curiously. Then he brought himself back to the present sharply.

"You are now convinced," he went on calmly, looking at her with a quiet smile, "that he didn't kill your husband ?"

She nodded calmly.

"What made you think he had ?"

"Oh, I don't exactly know. But I just thought he might have done, when Hicks said there was a gentleman here, and described him. You see, I wrote to him — in Africa — begging him to come back. I couldn't stand it any longer. I didn't know he was in town until that afternoon, and I . . . I was frightened. That's really all."

"No. What else ?"

I saw that Lewis of course had noticed as well as I her barely perceptible hesitation.

"Nothing else," she said.

They looked at each other steadily for some seconds.

"But you are definitely sure now that it was not he ?"

"Definitely, Major Lewis."

"Do you know Mr. Maitland-Rice ?"

She looked surprised at that, then smiled whimsically. It was the first sign of the old Catherine I'd seen for some time.

"We've discussed chrysanthemums across the garden wall once or twice. I should have known him well, I suppose, because he's down near us a good deal. I know Margaret Norland, whom he is to marry. Her father is the rector in the village near us, and Father's oldest friend. They're quite wealthy, and Margaret is a lovely creature, a sort of Venetian-glass person. But I actually know very little of him. He's a strange, nervous little man."

"You've never heard anything against him ?"

She raised a puzzled face to his, and her lip curled ever so slightly.

"Nothing, Major Lewis. I'm not interested in people's skeletons. I remember one morning, a year ago, after Mr. Maitland-Rice and I had talked about a swallow that was nesting in our eaves — he's an ornithologist — I met my husband downstairs. He had been watching us talk across the wall, and he made some sneering remark. I'd better be careful, or something of the sort. But he could always tell you something unpleasant about anyone."

She stopped, and looked inquiringly at him.

"Now please tell me about the diamond."

"I have nothing else to tell you about it, Major Lewis," she said firmly.

"Ah well," he replied with a smile, "we'll let it go, and I'll tell you about it in a day or so."

She looked at him steadily as she went out through the door which he held open for her.

"Come along, Braithwaite !" he said then, energetically. "No sloth ! We've got a job to do before we see Boyd."

Again we were in a taxi hurtling across the town.

This time, however, I recognized the way to Shepherd's Bush.

"Had you ever been out here before yesterday, Braithwaite ?" Lewis asked. I assured him that I had never in my life been in the district, so far as I knew.

"Queer," he said, "what orbits people get settled into in town, isn't it ?"

We stopped in front of Talbot's house; but Lewis, to my surprise, went up the stairs of the house next door and rang the bell. It was immediately answered by the old person we had encountered the day before. She was apparently going out — she had a hat and coat on — and to my amazement Lewis came down with her and helped her into our cab.

"This is Mrs. Maxwell, Mr. Braithwaite," he said. "She's coming to help us in a little experiment."

I suddenly felt ill. Was that what he had been playing with Catherine for ? My brain hammered in my head and I didn't hear a tenth of the woman's constant chatter.

We drew up before the district police station. I was more bewildered than before. Had Boyd arrested Catherine ? Was that why Lewis had taken me away ? The man Tate was there waiting for us. He handed Lewis a small satchel, and the sergeant, who evidently expected him, took him into a rear chamber, leaving me with that hateful woman.

After a little Lewis returned and beckoned us to follow. Oddly enough, a great weight fell from my shoulders when we entered the room. We were in the mortuary; it was evidently not Catherine we were dealing with. Lewis lifted a sheet; we saw the body of a young woman, with dark hair, over which a black hat had been placed. I looked at him in astonishment; but our friend from Shepherd's Bush spoke up eagerly.

"Aye, that's her !" she said, wagging her head ominously. "That's Mrs. Talbot, the poor dear !" She shook her gaunt head like an old crow.

Lewis carefully removed the hat, and looked inquiringly at her again.

"Aye, aye. That's the one. That's her the same. I seen her often."

She was led out by the sergeant, asseverating the fact to all interested; and Lewis, touching my elbow, quietly removed the dark hair from the body. It concealed the flaxen hair of Mimi Dean.

Without giving me a chance to speak — which I was incapable of doing, in any case — he hurried after his witness. I followed along, very glad to be out of that room. In the sergeant's room Lewis drew out a photograph.

"Who's this, Mrs. Maxwell ?" he asked. "Ever see him ?"

I saw that it was Scoville. But Mrs. Maxwell's face showed only a disappointed morbid curiosity. "I dunno, sir," she said regretfully.

It was pleasing to see that she did not know everyone. The photograph of Scoville made no impression at all upon her. But this, I thought, still left unsolved the identity of Mr. Talbot. Could it be Maitland-Rice?

I saw then that Lewis had produced another photograph. I looked at it over the woman's head. The person was strange to me. He wore a bowler hat and dark mustache, and little patches of grey showed at his temples. Mrs. Maxwell, however, gave a pleased and greedy bleat of recognition.

"Ah!" she said instantly. "That's him — and the other was her! Mr. and Mrs. Talbot!"

I have no doubt the woman had every belief that she was hanging him in those words.

"Thank you," Lewis said affably. He retained his usual urbanity, but I could see that he was very much satisfied with something. He despatched the voluble creature into the taxi and off to Shepherd's Bush with superhuman tact and firmness, and stood looking silently after her for a moment. Then he turned to me.

"Well, there we have it, Braithwate," he said with a whimsical smile. "Here's Mr. Talbot. Mimi Dean was his alleged wife."

"But who, in Heaven's name, *is* it?" I demanded.

He held up the photograph and contemplated it with a sober smile. "It's not a very pleasant reve-

lation," he said. "A photographer touched this up
for me. He added, at my direction, a mustache
and a bowler hat, with a little dignified grey at the
edges of the hair. And there we have Mr. Talbot
— or Nelson Scoville."

CHAPTER FIFTEEN

WE RETURNED at once to Moreton Gardens, where Boyd met us. My mind was in a whirl as I tried to fit this revelation into the idea that I had formed of things.

"There's no doubt of one thing," Lewis was saying. "That is, that Scoville and Miss Dean, disguised as the Talbots, have carried on an extensive business in blackmail for four or five years. It's chastening thought. It shows the fallacy, Richard, of the theory that one can't hide in London. Look at that business in Torquay. The man changed his name and carried on an elaborate swindle not a hundred yards from where he was wanted for another fraudulent operation. He had to commit suicide before it came out. At that, it was just in time to prevent him from involving a rather decent girl in a bigamous relationship."

"But the police," I said. "Surely that thing can't go on for five years ?"

"The police aren't involved, my dear sir," Lewis said. "When they are, of course something happens. But the ordinary law-abiding citizen can go out of his door in the morning as Smith, enter a house around the corner of the average London square as Brown, and no one the wiser. Unless he's found dead in one or the other of his houses some morning.

"Here's an instance. Early in the last century a man left home one morning and didn't turn up for eighteen years. His wife moved from her home in Jermyn Street, after a while, to a smaller place. The husband got acquainted with a baker who lived across the street from her. He called on the baker at least once a week and watched his wife from the baker's parlor window. No one knew a thing about him until he decided to return.

"No, I think, Braithwaite, that unless a man does something to attract police attention, he's fairly safe in London. How much do you know about the man whose flat is above yours ?"

I had to admit I knew nothing about him, not even his name.

"Another thing," he went on. "The simpler the disguise, the more convincing, and the less likelihood of anyone's spotting it. A mustache on a clean-shaven man, a bowler hat on a man who never wears one, dark hair instead of light — or with a woman just a different style of hair-dressing — is enough. The simplest thing is the most effective and the least likely to go wrong.

"Take the case of Scoville. I'm having Tate look into it, to make sure, but I think there's no doubt he never was abroad at all, except for a couple of weeks, perhaps, in the spring and summer. He was non-existent, as Nelson Scoville, of Moreton Gardens and Piccadilly. As N. V.

Talbot, an eccentric person of means, with a mustache, bowler hat, and greying hair — which I hit upon, by the way, from that hat he, or rather Mimi, left behind in Shepherd's Bush; there was a little white powder underneath the brim — you have a completely different person. Dress him in a ready-made misfit from Oxford Street instead of his twenty-guinea suit from Saville Row, and put him in Shepherd's Bush, and he could spend his life in London without anyone's being the wiser — unless, of course, he gives out his telephone number and gets himself murdered."

"But what about Miss Dean?" I asked.

"I have no doubt it was her idea, in the first place," he said. "She's an actress, and a clever one. More than that, I think it's obvious he was in love with her. She . . . well, she may have been with him; but they say women are shrewder than men about those things."

"Rot," said Boyd. "Have a drink."

"Be it so," Lewis replied. "And thanks, I will. Maybe it is rot, but I've yet to find a case where the Mimi Deans didn't hold the whip hand. Who called a truce in this business, my boy? It was Scoville, not Mimi."

"Called it a bit late," said Boyd, yawning openly. "Now, if you'll stop all this ghastly bilge you're emitting, I'll tell you an interesting tale of the bird-man in the Zoo."

"Surely . . ." I began.

"I call it that," Boyd interrupted me with a grin. Then he became sober. "Yes, I've had a long and heart-to-heart talk with Mr. Maitland-Rice. The Zoo is Park Lane and Shaftesbury Avenue and Shepherd's Bush, and the tiger is Mimi, and the jackal is friend Scoville — to take this amiable idiot's estimate of them. And, I may say, hearing Mr. Maitland-Rice is believing. He's really in a most beastly sweat."

"Go on," Lewis said.

Boyd told his story with more earnestness than I would have expected of him.

"Seven years ago," he said, "Maitland-Rice met Mimi at Brighton — people still went to Brighton seven years ago — and never having looked at a woman in all his thirty-six years except his mother, and his mother having got bumped off — died, Braithwaite, flu or something — he soon became at loose ends. Things got rather hot, in the American sense; too hot for Maitland-Rice. He thought marriage would be a sort of stabilator — if you know what I mean. [I was sure I didn't, but Lewis seemed to.] But Mimi wasn't having any. She knew far too much. So she up and goes to Paris, leaving him completely overwhelmed. Poor devil, it was the first fun he'd ever had, and of course he thought he was in love. He wrote the girl hundreds of letters, including those sad things we saw today.

"Well, she cannily saved the worst of them, and told him to go peddle his papers — as we say in America, Braithwaite."

"If you would confine yourself to English," I said, "we would have a much clearer idea of what you're trying to say.   At least, I would."

"Ah well, have it your own way.   It took Maitland-Rice about a year to get over it.   Then he met a certain Margaret Norland and soon became very intimate with her family.   She was everything that Mimi wasn't, and very much like Maitland-Rice's mother (jolly old Œdipus).   He saw his mistake then.   It took him years, I gathered, of devotion and gentle circumventing, as it were, to win Miss Norland who, from his confused account, is sort of fragile and spirituelle-like: if you two bounders can possibly understand me. Just a year ago she promised to marry him.   That rather surprised him, innocent and modest soul that he is; and he was more surprised, two days later, to get a letter, unsigned, with a hint of his affair with Mimi, and a simple request for £500.

"He wrote Mimi an indignant letter.   She denied any knowledge of the matter and said she'd destroyed all the letters, to the best of her knowledge. But he felt she was laughing up her sleeve — or where her sleeve would have been if she'd worn one, I suppose.   And that same day he got another letter, typed and unsigned, with an excerpt, not long but quite long enough, I gathered, from one of his more heated efforts. This letter gave a 'phone number — which you, my dear hearers, have already guessed. He called it, and after some conversation with Mr. Wills — so-called — sent the money to him, at an accommodation address.

"Then it went from bad to worse. Mimi after this refused to see him; and shortly after, Mr. Wills called up again. £1000 would prevent him from reluctantly sending a letter to Miss Norland."

"Why didn't the fool tell them to go ahead ?" I asked.

"Come, Braithwaite ! Don't be indelicate. If you'd read the letters . . ."

"But good heavens !" I said. "Dr. Norland . . ." I stopped abruptly. Boyd interrupted me.

"The rector," he said drily, "would not have been over-pleased with them either. No, he couldn't do that, of course. And I don't blame him. It's all very well to say academically 'Do your damnedest,' but it's another matter when you know too well how sanguinary their damnedest is."

Boyd drained a thoughtful glass.

"Let's get into the Christian era," Lewis suggested patiently. "What happened yesterday, for instance ?"

"Not so fast ! The best is to come. Maitland-Rice, the poor fellow, got into the habit of ringing up Shepherd's Bush, and each ring left him minus whatever they happened to think of. I say 'they,' because even he had no doubt, by that time, that

little Mimi was part and parcel. But of course he
didn't know who the man was and he couldn't find
out. He'd spotted Mr. Wills the grocer, but that
was as far as he got. Mr. Wills didn't look so evil
to him; he didn't know what more to do, and all in
all he was in a blue funk about the business, not having the foggiest about where it was going to end.

"And then, one terrible morning—so it seemed
to him—he looked out of his window, and saw a
lame albino swallow, crow, hawk, eagle, owl, or
something, on the Scoville's balcony. He wasn't
dressed, and he went to the telephone to ring up
Mrs. Scoville, whom he knew slightly, to ask her to
have Hicks bring the bird over to him. To his
complete and ghastly consternation, James Henry
Wills answered the phone. He nearly dropped
dead. And the whole thing then naturally dawned
on him. You see, although he'd rather suspected
all the time that Mimi was Scoville's mistress, he's
too decent a chap to suspect a member of his own
class of such swinery."

"When was all this ?" Lewis asked.

"Monday last, my boy. From then on he's a
little befuddled. He had several engagements and
went blindly through them. But this is a little
interesting and to the point. On Monday night he
was sitting in his room in the dark, watching the
windows across the wall, trying in despair to make
up his mind what to do. And he saw a woman —
he guessed it was Mimi — creep in the back gate and

hide in the shadow of the house. She went inside
in a few minutes, and after a little he saw her come
out again. That was about ten minutes later."

Lewis puffed more vigorously on his pipe and I
confess that my own heart beat a little faster.
This business of the murder, and the poisoning, and
the blackmail running all through it, was ghastly
enough; and the secret unseen watcher in the darkness in some way seized upon my imagination. It
seemed to me that the business was very grim and
abhorrent.

"That was *Monday* night, Richard?" Lewis
asked with great satisfaction. "Not Tuesday, eh?
That's a great help."

"Rather," Boyd said. I suppose I, as usual,
showed my complete lack of comprehension.

"Miss Dean's story," Lewis explained, "of her
being here Tuesday night, was false; she was here
Monday night; and *that*, by Jove, is when the
quarrel took place! I knew," he continued, "that
her story was false, because — among other things
— when she called up Wednesday morning, she had
no idea Scoville was dead. So we can put her story
— some of which was true, I think — just back one
day. Go on, Richard."

"Well, on Tuesday he tried to see Scoville and
couldn't. He went to his bird meeting and got
home about one o'clock or so. He got out his
revolver and started over. He'd got another
'phone call that day and was pretty desperate. The

rector wanted the wedding to take place next week. Well, he started downstairs, when he heard two gunshots, one almost immediately after the other, but not in instant succession. That brought him to, and of course he didn't know what might have happened. So he went back upstairs and went to bed.

"All the next day he tried to get in touch with Mimi, being pretty sure she still had the letters. He called at her house, wrote her offering £5000 — which he hadn't got — anything to get the letters. Then, in despair, he went around to Shepherd's Bush again. And later in the day, again; and he saw Mimi going away from the vicinity with a dispatch case. He guessed, in a vague way, that it contained the letters."

"So he tried then to get them at the theatre ?" Lewis said.

"Right. He couldn't get into her room, but if he had he wouldn't have got them. She was doing a new turn, in which she was the modern business girl or something, and carried the box around the stage with her. There's a little item about it in the theatre gossip this morning. A shrewd little woman, eh ? It was nip and tuck with them and she won. Up to a certain point, as one may say."

Somehow I couldn't help saying just then — it slipped out almost involuntarily — "What does it profit a man if he gain the whole world and lose his own soul ?"

Oddly enough, neither of them laughed.

CHAPTER SIXTEEN

LEWIS AND BOYD sat there smoking. Maitland-Rice's story had evidently given them food for thought. Why they always chose that room to sit in was beyond me, but they seemed to prefer it to the library. I may say I was not particularly at ease there. The figure of Scoville was never far out of my thoughts when I looked at that table, and today, while they were pondering over Maitland-Rice, his face seemed to interweave itself, in my mind, with the horrible, distorted image of Mimi Dean; and I could see her hands, straining out into the air. It was with a good deal of effort that I stayed there at all, I think. They were so calm about it that I felt I could hardly show any nervousness.

"You've a man tracing the chocolates?" Lewis asked after some minutes.

Boyd nodded.

"I think," Lewis continued, "that I'll see Hicks again. I'm very much interested in the matter of the burglar alarms; and don't you think it's a little strange about Scoville's man?"

"He hadn't any here," Boyd said.

"That's just the point," Lewis replied thoughtfully.

They summoned Hicks. I couldn't see that he

had much to offer. He repeated his story just as before, if a trifle more readily.

"Do you put on the burglar alarms every night ?" Lewis asked.

"Yes, sir. Every night."

"The doors as well as the windows are included in the circuit, of course ?"

"Yes, sir. Doors *and* windows."

"But of course, it's simple enough to disconnect the system ?"

"Only from inside, sir. The switch box is in the linen closet at the end of this hall. Only the people in the house know about it."

"So that if anyone came in, it would be with inside help ?"

Hicks stopped a moment. "Inside help" seemed to suggest something unpleasant to him. His deep-set eyes gleamed defiantly.

"If you mean, sir, that either Flora or me . . ."

"No, no, no," Lewis said, with some impatience. "I mean nothing of the sort. We've learned elsewhere that a certain person had access to the house by the rear door at night."

Hicks chewed his lips sullenly. "What was I to do about it ?" he said. "He had her come. I couldn't tell the mistress. He was a bad 'un with the women. I knew — " He stopped short.

"What did you know ?"

"Nothing."

"How long have you known Scoville ?"

The man looked at him suspiciously. "Since during the war."

"In the war?"

"Yes. He was a good soldier," he added.

"How long have you been with him?" Lewis continued.

"Near six years. When they came here to live."

"Did you valet him?"

"No. He had a servant; Thomas, his name was."

"Where is he now?"

"I don't know. He went with him last spring. That's all I know, except that he's a dirty, rotten scoundrel."

The suppressed fury behind the man's picture of the missing valet, which he delivered quietly enough, startled me, and I noticed that Lewis and Boyd were looking curiously at him. Lewis hesitated a moment. Then he dropped the subject of the valet and said suddenly, "Tuesday morning the burglar alarms were off."

Hicks is a bright enough fellow, but the transition was too much for him. He started in confusion before he realized what Lewis had said. Then he replied easily enough, "Tuesday morning they were. But I didn't mention it, because Flora said she thought she'd heard the mistress at the door herself. So of course I didn't say anything to her about it."

"And why didn't you mention that they were off Wednesday morning ?"

"Why, I . . ." The man stammered and was finally silent.

"They were off, then," Lewis said.

"Yes, they were off, all right."

"But you put them on 'Tuesday night ?"

"Yes, sir. And it weren't me or Flora that put them off."

"Then it must have been either Mr. Scoville, or Mrs. Scoville ?"

The man agreed cautiously, not seeing (as I didn't either) to what this was leading.

"There was no one else here ?"

"No, sir."

"What about Thomas ? Has he a key to the house ?"

This question struck fire. To my astonishment Hick's eyes narrowed (I had read about such a phenomenon but had not seen it until now) with hatred and fury, and his hands clenched.

"Yes," he said. "He's got a key. But he wouldn't dare come here, the ———."

"Why not ?"

"Because I'd kill him," he answered quietly.

Lewis was silent a moment. Then he said calmly, "Miss Flora ?"

"Who told you ?" Hicks cried. "Has that swine been around here ?"

"Come, come," Lewis said. "Are you engaged to her?"

"We're married," he replied.

"And Thomas, I suppose, was annoying to her?"

"You wait a minute."

Hicks went out of the room and returned almost immediately, leading Flora, pale but calm.

"Tell them about it," he said. It was evident that he was master in his own household.

So she told us the whole story quite directly.

"Thomas came here the year after we came," she said quietly. She was evidently prepared for this ordeal and was quite calm about it. "He wanted to marry me, and I liked him pretty well, only he couldn't marry me until he had a divorce, he said, but he said it was just the same before God and man, and that we were man and wife. He talked very fine phrases, he'd been with a writing gentleman. Then one day he said he needed money and tried to get me to borrow from Madam. He'd always ask me questions about her and I'd talk about her. I'd been with her so long, you know, since we were both twenty, in the country. He wanted to know about Mr. Davidson, too. Then one day he told me he'd stolen money from Madam but if I told he'd go and leave me. I was afraid of that."

She looked silently at Hicks.

"Then he began to steal from her all the time and said if I told he could prove it was me, and he'd tell

all I'd told him about her. I was worse afraid.
Then Mr. Hicks began to like me and it got different somehow.

"I told him I didn't care what he did and that I'd
tell Madam myself. Then last year the master
called me in here one night and told me that he
knew I'd stolen from Madam and that I'd . . . I'd
lived with Thomas. He tried to make me sign a
paper he had.

"He said it was an agreement with Thomas to
make him marry me. I just got a glimpse of it,
though, and I saw Mr. Davidson's name in it. I
knew it was something tricky and I said I wouldn't
ever sign it. He wouldn't let me go, and then
Thomas came in, and they said they'd prove I was
a thief, and they'd find some of Madam's jewelry
in my box. I was afraid of the way they looked
and I knew a girl wouldn't have any chance after
that."

She stopped a moment.

"What did you do ?" Lewis asked gently.

"I went and told Madam the whole thing, like
Hicks said to do. I'd told him about it because he
wanted to marry me and so I had to tell him to be
honest."

"Wiser than most," Boyd said softly.

"And she knew I wouldn't lie to her. She said
she'd see about it and for me not to be afraid.
And then Mr. Scoville and Thomas went to France.

"That's all."

Lewis shook his head. "The other night?" he said.

She went pale. "I don't know what you mean!" she cried. Up to this point she had been calm enough but there was more than a suggestion of hysteria now.

"Yes, you do. Tuesday night?"

"Tell them," Hicks ordered abruptly as she looked from one to the other of us with frightened eyes.

"After Mr. Davidson had left," she said. "I'd been down talking with Hicks. I met Mr. Scoville. He'd just let him out. He said Thomas was back and could prove I'd married him, and he was going to have me arrested for bigamy. Oh, it's too awful."

She sobbed quietly.

"Then he said I was to get Madam's revolver — I was to be careful not to touch the handle — and give it to him."

There was silence in the room.

"Did you tell Hicks?" Lewis asked.

"No, he was in the basement stairway and heard it."

"Did you tell Mrs. Scoville?"

"Yes. I was afraid for her."

"What did you do?"

She looked around her hysterically.

"I went in Madam's room. We locked the doors and sat up together by the fire all night."

"All that night, until morning ?" Lewis asked quickly.

"Yes."

"And it was there that you heard the revolver shots ?"

"Yes."

"What else did you hear ?"

"There wasn't a sound else," she answered solemnly. "We were terribly scared. I was, at least. And so we didn't dare go out. But we didn't hear a single other sound."

Lewis looked steadily at her. Then he turned to Hicks. "And you ?" he said.

"After I'd told the blackguard what I thought of him, I went to bed," the man replied harshly. "And that's the truth."

Lewis leaned forward.

"Hicks," he said, "you knew Scoville in the war. You knew he shot with his right hand !"

CHAPTER SEVENTEEN

IT TOOK some time after that to explain to an incredulous Boyd that although Scoville was ordinarily and naturally left-handed, he ate, played golf, and shot right-handedly. I believe this is not an uncommon phenomenon; in fact, two instances of such partial ambidexterity, if it can be called so, have occurred in my own acquaintance.

Hicks and Flora were dismissed at the arrival of the man Boyd had set to trace the chocolates responsible for the death of that ill-fated girl. The manufacturer's name was, of course, on the box, which was an exceedingly elaborate one. The chocolates had cost, I believe, forty shillings. By good fortune, the shop at which they had been bought had been easily and quickly located. The man had gone first to the main branch in Piccadilly, and then, as a likely place, to the branch nearest Scoville's home, in the Old Richmond Road near South Kensington station. And there he had found it.

We went there now and interviewed the shop-assistant. She remembered the box very well. The gentleman who had bought it, she told us, was evidently not in the habit of doing such things. She smiled with some condescension as she told us how he had come in and pointed to an elaborate box in the window, saying he would take that along. It was only a dummy box, of course, and she hadn't a filled one in the shop. Rather than lose a forty-shilling order, she persuaded him to wait, as he declined to allow her to send it, while she packed the box from her trays.

She remembered the box distinctly because it had been in the window for some time and was slightly faded. ' The gentleman could see if they'd look across the corner. There was a faint line of color showing that something had protected part of the box from the rays of the sun. She was not, however, able to describe the gentleman who bought the box, other than by saying he was a gentleman, oldish, quiet, and sort of ordinary-looking. She glanced from one to the other of us.

"More like that gentleman, I mean, than either of you."

Boyd and Lewis smiled, to my exceeding discomfort. It's annoying to be described as oldish and ordinary-looking, even by a shop-assistant. Boyd was unable to resist referring to the incident for some time, and quite foolishly, no doubt, I always experienced the acutest vexation at it. I suppose, as I explained to him, we are all rather sensitive about allegations of mediocrity.

We took our departure after further efforts to make the girl more definite in her description. There seemed no doubt in Lewis and Boyd's minds that the description fitted Maitland-Rice as well as such a description, or lack of one, could do. It was similar, too, to that given of him by Molly, the maid at Park Lane.

"I think," Lewis remarked as we got into a taxi and drove off down town, "that Mr. Maitland-Rice is definitely our leading entry. Hicks might have shot Scoville, but he hasn't the finesse to cover it up. He'd have taken the boat train for Paris, and we'd have had him at Boulogne. Besides that, he has nothing against Miss Dean, and couldn't remotely have had anything to do with the bon-bons. On the other hand, Maitland-Rice obviously has greater cause to fear Scoville than Hicks had, plus the cause, and the opportunity, or at least means, of doing in Mimi. We can't be positive, of course, about the chocolates until your man takes the girl around to see him. And of course, there is every possibility that it was Mr. Talbot who got the chocolates."

Boyd shrugged. "I don't so far see any way out for Maitland-Rice. He's a crack shot, by the way."

"How does he happen, incidentally, to live by the Scoville's?" Lewis asked. "Any design there?"

"Pure accident. He was there years before they were. Both properties were bought from the Norlands. Maitland-Rice's by his mother, the Scovilles' by the old lord. Norland had a lot of town property, but can't be bothered with it. And having pots of money he didn't have to be. It's quite simple."

"What is his address, by the way ?" Lewis asked.

I supplied it, rather wondering if he planned to upset poor Maitland-Rice's apple-cart himself. If the man were seriously anxious not to have his name mentioned in certain quarters, it seemed to me rather curious procedure on the part of a private agent to interview the very persons involved.

"I'm starting a search for Mr. Thomas," Boyd said. "He ought to be able to give us enough evidence to . . ." He allowed his sentence to trail off ominously.

"I very much doubt if you'll find him," Lewis said seriously. "If you do, you can't have a more likely witness. I don't quite like the looks of his absence."

Boyd shrugged his shoulders in dismissal of the notion that he might be anxious for the outcome. We lapsed into one of those silences in which the two wrapped themselves, leaving me utterly at a loss to know what they were thinking, if, indeed, they were thinking any thing.

"If Maitland-Rice bought the box of chocolates, Richard," Lewis said suddenly, "how did he get them to Mimi's place ? The doorman told me they came through ordinary channels. I supposed him to mean they were delivered by hand. No one remembers the messenger. We'll just stop by *The*

Times office and put a line in the agony column."

"'AJAX: *Who delivered the poisoned chocolates ?*
— HECATE.' " Boyd said. "Your simple faith isn't
up to Norman blood, or whatever the poet says,
my boy."

His banter failed to stop Lewis. When he came
out of *The Times* he gave the driver directions I
did not hear.

"Out you get, Richard," he said then. "Get a
cab of your own. Find out about those two pass-
books; also Mrs. Scoville's. We'll see you at dinner
at my place. Eight o'clock."

Boyd left, after some of their usual exchange of
broad pleasantries, and we crossed Waterloo Bridge
and wound in and out of the purlieus of Camberwell until we came to a small public-house called
The Old Pack Horse; which, I learned from the
proud sign on the door, was a free house, directed
by one William Mutton.

We went in. Mutton was out, but his wife was
pleased to be of service. The house was closed,
of course, and she invited us into a small back parlor, redolent, it seemed to me, of centuries of beer
and spirits. Many a back and side, as Lewis remarked afterwards, had doubtless gone bare to
bring the place to so rich a state.

Lewis opened with a volley of beguilements that
the woman found irresistible, and before long,
quite forgetting the rôle of the discreet publican's
wife — if there really is such a rôle — she was tell-

ing us about her clients. She remembered one
night when Hicks was there, and asked about some
customers. They had been talking, two of them
whose names she had forgotten, to a gentleman
whom Hicks had recognized. Now Hicks was a
crony of Mutton's, and his friends were hers.
Hicks's friends as well, she indicated generously, had
claims upon her. We were duly registered. Hicks
wanted to know what the two were up to. Well,
she couldn't of course say. When your house is
in Camberwell you takes the bad with the good.
But they was rare bad 'uns. Made a living off
servant girls, as like as not; and furnished information, she suspected, for shrewder people to use.

Thomas ? Aye, he had been there with the
stranger Hicks had recognized. She knew nothing about him. Whenever he came, or whenever
the gentleman came, and sometimes they were together, they turned over a bit of money to the
boys. They always laughed and had a drink to
"the Ladies." She felt it was not above-board;
but what do you expect ?

Lewis asked her casually how much Hicks made
out of it. She was bewildered and then indignant.
Hicks had nothing to do with them others, and if
the gentleman was there he got out at once. There
was plainly nothing shoddy or interested about her
defence of the man; if she was as loyal to all Mr.
Mutton's friends they are more fortunate than
most. Lewis thanked her politely for her pains,

and we made our way through fetid streets filled
with appalling débris into the comparative purity
of Camberwell Road.

We were half-way across the bridge when Lewis
spoke. "This is one of the loveliest views in London, Braithwaite. In the world, if you're insular
enough."

Before I could think of a suitable comment he
went on.

"The only trouble is that we're all wrong.
There are deep roots and tangled motives in this
case. I thought at first that it was very simple.
I still think part of it is; but when you get two or
three simple things interwoven, the result is pretty
complex sometimes. Well, come around to Bedford Square tonight and we'll have a bite of dinner.
I gave Boyd's sergeant a 'hunch' of mine. We'll
know by dinner time if it works, and perhaps we'll
have a few more stray bits to fit into the puzzle."

I found myself rather suddenly on the footpath,
and saw the taxi and Lewis shoot westward along
Holborn. I was in front of Staple Inn, where I
have chambers, although how Lewis knew it I
hadn't, as Boyd says, the foggiest.

I hardly knew whether to dress or not, in the
circumstances. Finally I decided that as I always
dress for dinner it would be rather far-fetched for
me to change my habits merely because fate had
thrown me in with a couple of policemen of sorts.
I was a little surprised, however, to see them also

faultlessly attired, and apparently completely oblivious of the fact that they'd been pottering about with the unsavory details (to say the least) of other people's affairs during the day.

Lewis has the first floor flat in one of the Queen Anne mansions in Bedford Square. It is charmingly furnished, the dinner was excellent; indeed, all through the earlier part of the evening I was totally unconscious of his profession and the nature of our acquaintanceship. He was simply a man of the world with a decent career of Winchester and Oxford and a very respectable family behind him. And about Boyd I felt the same, knowing his case was similar in a lesser degree — although his family are in the Baronetage.

We had dinner cosily in a small dining-room where a fire burned cheerfully in the grate. Here I had also a pleasant impression of the man, in his complete lack of ostentation. I could see that he knew good food, good wine, good tobacco, and, what is rare in England these days, good coffee. Yet he did not hold forth during the meal on the proper way to serve Dover sole or the degeneracy of lobster and champagne. While dining with him it isn't necessary to place the year and vineyard of every sip you take, or call out the chef to cavil over his Hollandaise, to show that you weren't (or were) brought up on fish and chips.

I may be rather rabid about it, but I've sat at many tables where every calory was so thoroughly gone into — its origin and present and future states — that I could have demanded a dish of tripe, except, of course, that that curious dish is now the height of fashion.

But I'm getting as far from my account of the murders at Moreton Gardens and Park Lane as we did that evening at dinner. It actually seemed we had all forgot completely about it, until after dinner, when we sat over coffee and cigars in Lewis's living-room in the pleasant semi-light. It seems, however, that they had talked about it before I came.

"It's mostly the unpleasant story of Thomas the valet," Lewis said.

"You found him?" I asked. Heaven knew what might turn on him.

"He did not," Boyd observed. "He left it for me to do. Knowing, of course . . ."

"Nothing of the sort," Lewis said. "It's your beastly greed for kudos. You could have sent the sergeant."

He turned more gravely to me. "They found Thomas, in the cellar of the Shepherd's Bush house. He was there, as a matter of fact, when we went through it yesterday. In fact, he's been there a couple of days, probably. Dead."

"Dead!" I exclaimed.

"Dead," Boyd repeated grimly. "Murdered. Shot in the back of the head twice and stuffed into a pantry in the cellar."

"But who ?" I asked in consternation. This business was becoming steadily more inexplicable to me, and more ghastly.

"We can only guess now," Lewis said. "We'll know in a day or so. But I think Flora told the truth when she said that Scoville wanted his wife's revolver — with finger-prints if possible, you remember. He wanted to use it to hurt her, do you see ? I suspect it was to be left beside Thomas."

"It clears up one thing, too," Boyd put in. "The girl at the sweet shop thinks she can identify Thomas, from a photograph, as the buyer of the chocolates."

"Then," I cried, "he bought them for Scoville !"

"Well, it's not quite so simple," Boyd said. "We've looked him up. Finger-prints happened to be on record. His name is Elmer Wilson. He spent fourteen months in Pentonville for blackmailing a young woman. He did a little stretch for stealing, in Dartmoor, and he spent a bit of his youth at Borstal. But that's not the best. The really choice gem about him is this: he was killed in the War ! Can you better that ?"

Boyd shook his head mournfully.

"But, gracious Heavens !" I said, "how did he get into Scoville's service ?"

"I think we can answer that, too," Lewis said. "He was Mimi Dean's husband."

That was too much for me. I could only stare at them.

"They were married in 1916. She was nineteen then, thirty-one now. She was dancing in a low night club, before her rise to comparative fame."

"She must have worked hard to drag that dead weight upward," Boyd observed.

Lewis nodded. "Unless, of course, he supplied the ideas and the clients, so to speak. We might find that he knew Maitland-Rice, for instance."

"Ah yes," Boyd said. "The jolly old sparrow took lantern slides down to Borstal every Christmas, and little Elmer, the up and coming lad, ran the machine. Oh, it's just a step between everything and everything else, Braithwaite," he added solemnly.

"Shut up and don't interrupt," Lewis said imperturbably. "Scoville left the Shepherd's Bush place on Thursday to go to France. At least, Mr. Talbot was there Wednesday and not since, and Scoville certainly came from Boulogne on the Sunday boat. Boyd has traced him from the Crillon, where he spent Friday and Saturday nights — as Scoville — to London. Mimi Dean — as Mrs. Talbot — was at the Shepherd's Bush place after Thursday. In fact, of course, she was there yesterday when she took that dispatch case from the desk in the upper room."

"But who," I asked, "killed the man ? All this doesn't seem to get us anywhere ?"

He smiled a little patiently.

"It gets us just here, Braithwaite. Either Miss

Dean killed her husband, or Scoville did it.   And, either her husband or Scoville may have killed her by sending poisoned sweets.

"Mimi may have had more interest in Scoville than Thomas bargained for, for instance; or Scoville may have learned that Thomas was Mimi's husband, which I'm persuaded he didn't know when Thomas was his servant.   At any event, either one may have been jealous enough to kill. Scoville — Thomas, or Thomas — Mimi; or both. One thing is certain: it wasn't Thomas who killed Scoville.   He was dead at least a day before Scoville was shot.   Or, Scoville and Mimi may have been in a conspiracy, of course," he added thoughtfully.

"Dog eat dog," Boyd said callously.

"And I think it settles another thing, Richard," Lewis continued.   "Let's have the dispatch case. I think we now have some new light on the blackmail."

I thought of a pun, but didn't feel quite free to indulge myself.   Boyd would be quite intolerant.

CHAPTER EIGHTEEN

BOYD brought the dispatch case from a table near the door. Lewis took out a packet of letters, and reading each one through carefully, often several times, passed them across to Boyd, who in turn went carefully through them. Beyond seeing that they were typewritten on ordinary octavo paper, I took no part in the proceeding, until Boyd handed one — carefully chosen, I felt — to me.

"Let's have your opinion, Braithwaite," he remarked; too casually to pretend even remotely that he thought my opinion of any value.

"You can see," he went on calmly, "that these were written by a person not very familiar with the typewriter. Notice the rather erratic spacing, and the heavy letters and punctuation. The ribbon is new and so is the machine. It's a Corona, I should judge; the portable type."

"He got all that from the expert at Scotland Yard, Braithwaite," Lewis remarked without malice. "So don't be impressed. — Is that all he could tell you?"

Boyd nodded good-naturedly.

"Not very helpful. I can add something to that myself."

"Meaning," Boyd asked, "that he, she, or it, wasn't highly educated and needed money?"

I thought I saw a faint twinkle in Lewis's eye as he nodded.

"Ah well," Boyd rejoined, "lack of education is easy to imitate. I do a rather good thing in that line myself."

"Quite," Lewis agreed. "Well, let's get back to Thomas. I don't quite get him into the picture yet. It's certain he was dead before Tuesday ?"

"That's positive."

"What about the pass-books, then ?"

Boyd consulted his notes.

"Elmer Wilson, otherwise Thomas," he said, "has £890 to his credit at the Midlands Provincial Bank; Mimi — rather Mamie Wilson — has £200 cash, at the same bank, and investments, mostly in American motor stocks, amounting to £12,000.

"And your other tip was good. Wilson had a safe box at the bank. I got these out of it. Kept them for a little surprise."

He produced a packet from his pocket and handed it to Lewis with a gesture of triumph.

"By Jove !" Lewis exclaimed. For once he made no attempt to conceal his interest. "So he was leaving too. And Scoville, my boy, wasn't ! Now what do you make of that ?" He held over a new passport for my inspection.

Boyd stared at him.

"What makes you think so ?" he demanded.

"Observation, my dear fellow. Scoville's passport, which you'll remember we found in his table at Moreton Gardens, expired the day before he returned from France. I looked up the emigration officer who passed him. He remembered the case. He called Scoville's attention to the fact that the passport had expired the previous day. Scoville said he'd intended returning the day before, but had been ill or something, and that he'd now get a new one at once. Naturally the officer let him through. But — as I ascertained by application through the proper channels — no application was made for a new one."

"Hadn't much time, of course," Boyd observed drily.

"Time enough, if he was planning on a sudden departure," Lewis said. "So Mimi, née Mamie, used the box too." He held out the bank receipt for their joint use of the safe box.

We smoked a while in silence.

"I think," Lewis said, "that all this places our friend Thomas clearly enough. This is probably what happened. Mind you, I don't insist on it, and some of it isn't particularly convincing."

Boyd emitted an inarticulate, but I judged derisive, snort.

"It's the old, old triangle, I fancy," Lewis continued equably. "Elmer Wilson was a skunk of sorts, and Mamie was his wife. Scoville was one too, of a slightly different hue — should I say scent ? — and in love with Mamie as Mimi Dean. I suspect that Wilson supplied her with victims from the time of their marriage. We'll have to find out from Maitland-Rice if he had any connection with the man."

"Perhaps Mimi did her own touting, in his case."

"Perhaps. They must have been at the game some time, of course, to get together a clear £12,-000. However, the point is that Mimi, with the help of her husband, so involved Scoville, very cunningly, I fancy, that he couldn't get out of it. She probably led him on to pretty heavy expense, getting most of his allowance from the old lord and demanding more, and at the same time showing him how he could get it. I think a man of Scoville's training would stick at blackmail at first.

"Then as Talbot — Mimi's practical working out of her husband's plan — he got so involved as never to get free. And then Thomas, valet and apparent cat's-paw, whom we can be sure was clever enough to stay in the background, began to blackmail Scoville."

"Do you mean these letters?" I asked, pointing to those in front of Boyd.

He nodded.

"Those letters. At first I thought they were Scoville's own, to be sent out, or that had been sent back. They threaten too specifically. First, general exposure. That might be anyone. But then, they threaten with furnishing his wife evidence to divorce him. And that, of course, is Scoville. These letters were written by someone who knew

Scoville's identity with Talbot, the terms of his father's will, and the character of his wife. Thomas knew all three. So far as I can find out, he never even attempted to approach Mrs. Scoville in any way other than as a servant. He was apparently conscious of her general superiority."

"You mean he had nothing to blackmail her with," Boyd commented.

"Yes. Though he tried hard enough to get something. I thought until this evening that he was perhaps the barrel-organist whom she saw in Chiltern. But if he was dead, he more or less obviously wasn't playing barrel-organs. However, assuming that he has been getting a thousand a year from Scoville for the last four years, that helps to explain how he and Mimi have twelve thousand and Scoville nothing."

All this wretched business was becoming more terribly clear to me each moment.

"And Scoville, I think," Lewis continued, "learned some of this."

Boyd looked up in amazement.

"I've been guilty, I must confess," Lewis went on, "of a misdemeanor. I found this scribbled on the back of Scoville's own pass-book at Moreton Gardens. It's still there, by the way, for the police to see if they like."

He grinned at Boyd and handed him a slip of paper. I bent across the table and read on it "E. Wilson. M. P. B. 890. Bristol 1916."

"I hit on the bank account from the first, and the marriage with Mimi from the last — after several hours thought and a dozen false starts. I don't know when it was written. I imagine a day or two before Scoville shot Wilson, alias Thomas. I suspect he thought that with Thomas safely out of the way Mimi would be his, and that a quarrel — we heard of the last echoes of it at the Hot Pot Club — was her last word — but one — on the subject. She'd probably told him she was leaving him, and that she and Thomas were going to America. I judge that from her stocks, and this passport, which was issued, I see, the same day as hers, and has a consecutive serial number.

"Scoville's position was this. He'd lost the woman he loved, he'd more than lost his wife and, worse than that, he was at the mercy of two people whom he must have known to be entirely unscrupulous. That, I think, is when he shot Thomas."

"But ye Gods !" Boyd said softly; "then he poisoned Mimi, too !"

Lewis shrugged. "He gave her another chance."

We stared at him.

"If he sent the chocolates, he sent them on Monday. Only the bottom layer was poisoned. She was at his house after their quarrel Monday night. He must have made a very handsome offering."

"But he had nothing to offer," I said. "You've just proved that he was worse than ruined."

"Not with Thomas dead and Mimi with him. As for an offering — he may have had something in reserve. In fact, there was her life. Held in a two-pound box of chocolates. What more could he offer?"

"But if he had done . . .?" Boyd, I thought, was as mystified by all this as I was.

"I don't say he did. I was merely saying that he had something to offer her. If she refused him, he was completely shattered; he probably was cautious enough at the end."

Boyd and I sat there trying to grasp the implications of this terrible story.

"But you've no proof for it," Boyd said. "You can't prove that Thomas wrote the letters."

"The typewriter," Lewis suggested.

"You can't trace it."

"I have traced it, my boy. It's the portable Corona in Scoville's room. Where he was found dead. I wrote this on it at six o'clock this evening."

He handed Boyd a piece of paper with several typed sentences.

"Thomas," he went on, while Boyd rapidly compared the types, "is the only person who doesn't know how to type, who had the requisite knowledge, and the inclination, who had access to that machine over a period of several months."

"But good God, Monk! Don't you see where this leads to ?"

"Quite," Lewis replied calmly.

"To suicide !" I said suddenly, realizing the drift of these new facts so suddenly and dramatically put together.

They both looked at me. "To suicide," Lewis said; "or — to Mimi Dean."

CHAPTER NINETEEN

THE morning brought the inquests, which I have always particularly loathed. In the case of Mimi they brought in a verdict of murder by person or persons unknown. The analysis showed twenty grains of arsenic in her stomach and indicated that death had probably taken place in about ten minutes. That the poison had been introduced by means of the chocolates was established. The matter was left at that in the hands of the police.

Almost no evidence at all was taken in Scoville's case. Flora, Catherine, and I were called, questioned perfunctorily, and then excused. It was evident that the police were giving out no information. The inquest was adjourned for a week.

The press of course were not so easily satisfied. The young cub who'd followed me about since the day after Scoville's death pounced on me again as I left the court with Catherine and her father.

"Ghastly crowd, these people," Lord Chiltern muttered, as a dozen cameras clicked.

I stopped, of course, to get rid of the young leech from the *Daily Call.* He was more than my match, and I'm afraid I should have blurted out too much of the business if Lewis hadn't come to my rescue.

"Whatever you print about this business will be

libel," he said, amiably but firmly. The man made a wry face and shook his head.

"Have to keep faith with the great British public," he grinned. "Boyd hasn't given us a scrap, and the crumbs from the Hot Pot are running out."

"Try more free insurance and wait a bit," Lewis remarked drily, and dragged me away.

"I didn't see you at the inquest," I said, as we got into his car.

"I was there. There's been a general set-back in both cases. That's what it amounts to. And as the police don't want to have to back down on anything, they're not saying anything to have to back down on. All very simple."

"What *is* the set-back ?" I asked incredulously. "It seemed to me you'd unearthed hundreds of things. Enough to solve fifty cases."

"Well, that's more or less the point. The indications we've found point in different directions. That's the trouble. We're getting confused with our excess wealth of information. As a matter of fact, I've got Boyd to ask one of his superiors at the Yard in, to sort of give us a hand. Man name of Harper. He's had a lot of experience."

I stared at him; but apparently he was quite in earnest.

At his office we found a person waiting in answer to the advertisement Lewis had put in *The Times*. He was a typical street messenger, about sixty years old, I imagine, and seedy. The license on his sleeve was, to my mind, the only thing very responsible looking about him. He answered to the name of Doolan.

"It was me, sir," he explained with some pompousness. "My old woman saw your ad. She's a great one for the news, and I'd told her about me taking a parcel to Park Lane to Miss Dean the actress by way of business, and she saw about the lady's dyin', and says it was likely me that did it, in a way of speakin'. She's been watchin' the papers since yestiddy and she saw it."

Lewis, listening attentively, stemmed the rising tide at this point.

"You delivered a parcel to Miss Dean ?"

"The same, sir. As I was —"

"When was it ?"

"Monday evening it was, sir; about ten o'clock. You see —"

"Just a moment, please. Who gave it to you ?"

"Now that's 'ard to say, sir."

Seeing that we must have this in the man's own way, Lewis offered no further resistance.

"I was standin' at my post — at Redcliffe Square, where I'm always to be had *reliable*. I was talkin' to Potts, a taxi driver. I says, 'Potts, it's been a fair bad day.' Potts nodded to me. 'E don't say much, Potts. Silent-like."

We nodded in full comprehension.

"Just then I heard a whistle, sharp-like. I says,

'I'll go see if it's you as is wanted, Potts' and Potts
'e grunted. So I went along. But it wasn't for
Potts, it was for me !"

He tidied the front of his waistcoat complacently. It was evident that he was not often the
centre of affairs.

"It was for *me*," he repeated. "A tall, large
gentleman, and 'e 'ad on a dark overcoat. 'E says,
'Take this parcel to Miss Mimi Dean, 68 Park Lane,'
and 'e gave me two arfcrowns, and I did. And
that's the story, mister."

We looked a little amazed, I fancy, at that
abrupt ending.

"Well, what was he like ?" Lewis said encour-
agingly.

"There, now. That's what my old woman
asked. What's 'e like, she says only last night, and
I says, there you are, 'ow can I tell ?"

He seemed conscious of a certain failure in this
matter.

" 'E was biggish, but it was at the right side of
the square, where I meets him, coming away from
the top of the road. There's but one light there,
and it was pretty dark-like, so's I couldn't make
out well what 'e was like."

He screwed up his face to the difficult task of
explanation. "In my business, I gets a lot of messages to be delivered at night to ladies like that one.
Actresses. Don't want too much lookin' into.
You see, my beat is *respectable,* and respectable

gentlemen, they don't want it in the papers when they sends messages by night. I'm not the one to be nosey. As I says to Potts, 'I'm not the one to be nosey.'"

"Quite," Lewis said with fine self-control. But I could see he was rather vexed. "Well, how big was he? Was he about my size. Or as big as this gentleman?"

He motioned me to stand up, which I did.

The man shook his head decisively. "Ah, 'e was bigger, 'e was, and broader too. But not the size of you, mister."

"Well, was he old or young?"

"Middle, sir. Though as I didn't get the chance to tell, I makes a point of keepin' me 'ead down and not lookin' too much, when a gentleman gives me five bob. If I don't look 'im over too careful, then 'e'll call me again, 'e will. It's my way of *business,* you see?"

Lewis gave him five bob, but beside making him more willing and much more garrulous, it had no effect. Apparently the odd creature really did keep his eyes down and make a point of not looking at his customers, especially men who chose secluded parts of his square for their transactions. Lewis plied him with questions, but the voice, size, age, and general appearance of the man remained as vague as those of the buyer of the chocolates. With the exception, not very confidently held, that he was bigger than I and not so big as Lewis.

"Well," Lewis sighed, when the man had gone, "that was rotten luck. We've run into the very discreetest member of a discreet profession. Besides knowing that a largish gentleman gave Doolan the poisoned chocolates at ten o'clock Monday night, we're exactly where we were. And I needn't point out to you that as you aren't especially large, and as I'm rather too much so, that may mean almost anybody. It may have been Mr. Talbot, that is, or Thomas, or Maitland-Rice."

The telephone jangled on his desk.

"The girl at Puller's has seen Maitland-Rice," he said when he had hung up. "She thinks he may be the person who bought the chocolates. But she's not sure. And Boyd probably managed to suggest to her what little opinion she has. That's the worst of our nondescript average Englishmen, Braithwaite. They dress alike, walk alike, talk alike, act alike, and in fact they *are* alike. But it seems she's not even certain now that it was Thomas. And neither are we for that matter, since he was dead at the time, more than likely."

Again the telephone rang. This time he was more animated. "Come along; Boyd's got the rest of Scotland Yard at the house," he announced. With amazing rapidity this slow and leisurely person scuttled me out of the room and into his car before I had managed to arrange my ideas to meet this new emergency.

As we passed through the outer room, his

secretary handed him a parcel. He partly un-
wrapped it in the car. "Ah, it's old Lord Scoville's
book," he said. "You didn't know he'd written
it ? I'm very much interested in quaint old lords
who have sociological theories."

CHAPTER TWENTY

BOYD met us in the hall at Moreton Gardens.

"I've got Harper and Slade upstairs," he said, looking quizzically at Lewis.

"You old devil, Monk," he went on. "I'd jolly well like to know what's up your jolly old sleeve. The old bull frog upstairs is croaking as if he owned the pond, as usual. Bucked up fearfully by having his advice asked. Oh well, it's on your head."

"Need a little new blood in the case," Lewis said vaguely, as we mounted the stairs.

" 'sblood enough already," retorted Boyd. "It's brains we need."

Chief Inspector Parker was so much of a type of police detective as to be almost a caricature. Sandy haired, walrus-mustached, with bushy eyebrows and enormous hands and feet, he dominated the scene. His bulky frame completely obscured the mouse-like little man who sat at one side of the room balancing his hat on his knees.

Lewis shook hands with them and turned to me. "Chief Inspector Harper and Mr. Slade, Mr. Braithwaite," he said. Harper's grunt was perfunctory enough, but Mr. Slade's lack of enthusiasm was appalling.

However, for all the attention the others paid him he might have been somewhere in the box room, balancing his hat as carefully there, his pale eyes scarcely bothering to fasten themselves on anything in particular. The Chief Inspector was not of his sort in the least. The Press would doubtless call him a human dynamo. His voice was extraordinarily husky, so hoarse that it made my throat ache in listening to him, as he rasped out his words with apparently painful effort. I've never heard a machine gun, but I fancy Mr. Harper is what a machine gun would sound like if it had an acutely bad throat.

"Since you saw me, Lewis," he boomed, "I've been thinking this business over. I've run into several new things."

Boyd looked solemnly at Lewis and lighted a cigarette.

"First place," he cocked his tufted eyebrow at Lewis, "there's Mrs. Scoville, your client. The case against her's circumstantial. Point is, is it circumstantial enough?

"She had motive enough and opportunity. They haven't lived together for five years — as man and wife," he added modestly, — "and it's pretty well understood that she hated him. Quite natural. Besides, she was afraid of him. She certainly had opportunity enough, now. She was in the house. But there's where she'd be expected to be. There's no actual evidence to prove she wasn't in bed asleep. As for the £600,000, she'd get that next month simply by divorcing him."

He pulled his grizzly mustaches and snapped out ferociously, "Won't wash! You couldn't get a jury to convict any pretty woman on that much."

"Quite right, Inspector," said Lewis. "And even if my client were an old crone, instead of one of the loveliest women in London, I don't think there's enough evidence to get very far on. All of it points somewhere else, as you say."

That neither Boyd nor I had heard him say any such thing apparently didn't affect the situation. If the Inspector was surprised he recovered instantly.

"That's right," he croaked complacently. "And as for him being murdered, that's a white horse of a different color."

"And taste," remarked Boyd, pouring a tumbler half full of whisky and passing it to him. Harper's voice, I thought, ceased to be a mystery. Whether he regarded the eventuality of Catherine's killing her husband as suicide, or as just punishment, I was not sure. Apparently, however, he distinguished it in some way from actual murder.

"Now this fella next door," he continued, "he had motive, but you can't shoot a man on motive alone. And there's no evidence that anybody came in the house. Hicks never put on the burglar alarms — that's the long and short of that — and he's not sure anybody else did either. If they were on nobody could get in unless they were let in, and if they weren't on it's no matter.

"As for Dean, the thing is turned around. There's no doubt in anybody's mind" — he included us in a stare, though none of us would have thought of disagreeing with him openly — "that the two murders are connected. In the case of Dean, Mrs. Scoville had motive. But not a very strong one, from what I gather. And she hadn't the opportunity. The fella next door had both, and plenty of them.

"Now in the case of Scoville, neither of them could have got near him, close enough to shoot those shots, without running danger of getting hurt. He's twice as big as the two of them. Besides, they'd have to walk on this carpet, and you both say nobody did."

He fixed Boyd and Lewis with a choleric eye.

"There were no footprints on the carpet when I came in the room," Boyd said promptly. "The maid had stopped outside the door. So had Mrs. Scoville."

"And none but policemen's when I came," Lewis confirmed.

"And nobody can fly," Harper continued, "not even your bird-fella next door." He gave out a throaty chuckle. "And the shot in the heart wasn't fired more than a couple of feet away."

The quiet little man by the book-cases started uneasily and cast an apprehensive glance at Harper.

"Well, now. Take the dead man. He was connected with Dean, and they had an establishment

in the Bush under the name of Talbot.   Blackmail
was their game.   Dean was married to this Elmer
Wilson.   We'll call him Thomas.   They were
planning to double-cross Scoville and clear out.
They had the money.   They'd cleaned Scoville
and were leaving him with the bag to hold while
they shipped.   That's what I read from the pass-
books and the safe deposit box and her American
stocks.

"Well, Scoville wasn't as big a fool as they
thought he was.   He got the wind up, and on
Monday — I guess it was after Thomas had bought
the sweets for him — he caught Thomas trying to
leave with the box of letters and shot him twice
in the back of the head.

"Well, next he had the woman to deal with.
He'd got Thomas out of the way and he thought
she'd come back to him.   Well, he told her what
he'd done about Thomas.   The maid at her place
says she was hysterical all Monday afternoon, and
Monday night they quarrelled.   Dean came here
to fix it up and heard Mrs. Scoville quarrelling
with Scoville.   She heard enough to know Scoville
didn't stand an earthly to get a penny of the £600,-
000 his father left them.   That was enough for
her.   She damn well didn't want him without the
money.   So she left him flat.   This is what she
heard."

Dramatically he produced an envelop and
clapped it down on the table.

208 IN AT THE DEATH

"Returned from Crédit Lyonnais when they saw about Scoville's death. It came to the Yard after you left this morning," he explained a little lamely, it seemed to me, to Boyd. It almost seemed that he had taken the case quite out of Boyd's hands.

The letter was from Catherine to Scoville, written on Friday last. It notified him very tersely that she intended to divorce him; that she was filing suit December first or earlier; that she had planned to wait out the six years so that he could decently share the money his father had left, but that in view of something she had just learned she intended to act at once.

Lewis read the letter and looked at Harper.

"Have you seen Mrs. Scoville about this ?" he asked.

"I have. She acknowledges the letter and the quarrel, but she won't say anything more."

"Very wisely too," Lewis observed calmly. "Were counsel present ?"

Harper flushed hotly at this. He was one of the men, I learned later, recently involved in the Hyde Park cases about methods of questioning witnesses.

"Did you know she was trying to divorce him, Monk ?" Boyd asked quietly.

"I didn't know it," Lewis replied. "I guessed that Braithwaite here wasn't telling everything he knew about the legal affairs. When Mrs. Scoville admitted that she had called Davidson back, I was

pretty sure what it meant. She's hardly the sort
to appeal to an old lover unless she's making a clean
break."

I was in a rather uncomfortable position. Major
Lewis had certainly never given me the slightest
reason to believe he felt I hadn't confided fully in
him.

"It was a professional secret," I explained, a little lamely, I'm afraid.

"Professional secrets have hanged many a man,"
Harper wheezed at me angrily. The twinkle in
Lewis's eye reassured me, however.

"Well, now," the Chief Inspector went on, a
little more amicably. "The lady and her husband
quarrelled Monday night. She gave him the ulti-
matum. Dean heard it. As I say, she was damn
well sure she didn't want him either. She'd have
to support him. So she quit *cold*."

He paused, and Lewis spoke up. "There's one
other point, Inspector, that will help your case, I
think. I saw Manson, the K.C., this morning, at
the suggestion of Lord Scoville, the dead man's
brother, you know. He was retained three weeks
ago by Scoville's creditors, who someway got wind
of the terms of the will. It was on the strength
of the will, to be settled in January, that Scoville
borrowed about £16,000. Manson went down to
see Lord Scoville last week and he, thinking everything was all right, confirmed the report. But it
seems the creditors had less faith in Mrs. Scoville's

generosity than the lord had. They knew more about Scoville too, and they began to worry. And then they got rumors of the divorce — it must have been from your office, Braithwaite — and got the wind up for fair. They were planning to take action on Wednesday. And this is the most important: Manson told me that he told Scoville so, when he met him somewhere Monday evening. They belong to the same club."

I was literally stunned at such a leak in my office. It convinced me of the entire untrustworthiness of clerks, although only two of them could have known about it. It also convinced me of the necessity of getting back to my own affairs, if this was the way they ran without me.

The Chief Inspector cut short my reply with a series of sharp clucking noises, which I took to indicate surprise, pleasure, and recognition of the importance of this new piece of evidence.

"Well, now," he croaked again. "Let's hear your piece, Slade."

As the little man looked up in almost a startled way, Lewis explained to me in an undertone that he was from the Fire Arms Department of Scotland Yard.

"I've examined the wounds on the body," he said peaceably. His gentle, tired voice was a great relief after the Chief Inspector's. Examining violent wounds, however, was the last thing in the world one would have expected him to be doing.

"I've come to certain conclusions." He stopped as though it weren't really worth going on with, unless we insisted.

"The first is, that both shots were fired at very close range. The one in the heart is conclusive enough. There is blackening and burning present to prove it. The one in the temple has left no such marks, which, however, is not conclusive of the contrary. It frequently happens that shots at close range leave no marks. I have tabulated the known cases in my report to the Chief. The bullet went straight through the heart and came through a remarkably clean wound under the left shoulder-blade, which substantiates my hypothesis.

"I fired the remaining four shots in the revolver with negative results against a piece of white chamois. I then fired two hundred and fifty of the same sort with the same revolver. Two of them left no traces of blackening or burning. It is in the nature of an accident, but not quite one, since it does happen enough times to be considered in every such case."

The little man stopped wearily and then continued.

"There are many examples of that sort of thing. Hubbard, for instance, has an example in point. A man was seen flourishing a revolver. He then sat down under some bushes; in a few minutes a shot was heard, and his body was found with a bullet-hole in the centre of the forehead. Everything

pointed to suicide,.but there were no powder-marks
on the wound. The four remaining shots were
fired at white targets at distances of three, eight,
eighteen, and thirty inches. In every case the tar-
get was blacked.

"Now, in the second place, neither of these
wounds we are considering would necessarily be
instantly fatal. I believe the wound in the heart
was inflicted first, and that in the temple, which
would cause unconsciousness, last. Death was
caused ·by internal hæmorrhage."

He stopped this time for so long a time that I
had begun to think he definitely was not going on.

"You may be interested in a case of the sort that
comes to my mind. A boy, nineteen, inflicted
four wounds on his own person. The first bullet
entered the forehead and after taking a circuitous
route, lodged in the middle of the left temporal
lobe. The second went through the sternum and
cut the left ventricle of the heart. A third entered the abdomen, the fourth the neck. He died
of hæmorrhage.

"Then there is on record the case of a student
who shot himself in the head, walked through a
long passage to his bedroom and shot himself in the
heart. And finally, there's a similar case of a policeman who, in the presence of witnesses, shot
himself through the head and then fired a shot
into his chest. He also died of internal hæmorrhage.

"My conclusions in the present case are not, therefore," he continued with less apathy than before, "as fanciful as you might think. In view of the evidence of the bullet-wounds, especially in connection with that of the rug and finger-prints, and the general lack of signs of struggle anywhere, I do not hesitate to state it as my opinion that Scoville committed suicide."

He came to a full stop.

"And, if I may be permitted to say so, I think also that in so doing he performed an act of service to Society."

CHAPTER TWENTY-ONE

IF I had expected Inspector Harper to gloat over his triumph over the younger man and the "private," I had underestimated him. Not for nothing had he risen by sheer force of ability and hard work from a constable's beat. He knew the ordinary criminal, I imagine, like a nursery rhyme; they were so much red tape to be got through with before they began their sentences. At this point in the present affair, he showed nothing but the most earnest desire, expressed in throaty shouts, to determine upon the correct solution of the appalling events of the past week.

"Let's forget all our fine theories now, and look at the evidence of this room," he rasped. "When you opened that door, Boyd, what'd you see?"

"Scoville hunched forward in his chair over the table, his right hand flung forward, a revolver a few inches from it," Boyd said calmly.

"Signs of disorder?"

"None. The body was in perfect order. The rug was just about as it is in that corner." He pointed to one end of the room where nobody had been recently. "It apparently hadn't been walked on much."

"Hmm . . . But the pile on this carpet is so

soft anyone might about as well walk in the snow, for leaving footprints."

Boyd nodded his assent.

"Then except for the finger-prints being right instead of left, there wasn't no direct evidence of murder ?"

"The two wounds," Boyd said, shrugging.

"Well, you got Slade's report on them."

"Quite," Boyd retorted, a little ruffled. "But Slade's just got around to giving his report this morning. In the circumstances I think I was justified in assuming it was a carefully planned murder."

"Yes, yes. I don't gainsay that. You've done pretty good work. The trouble with you young fellas is, you're always wanting things to be *complicated*. That's just where you're wrong. Life's not complicated, it's simple, and so's murders and criminals. I heard a philosopher fella at London University say one of the points about a hypothesis is parsimony. That's what you want, parsimony. The more parsimonious a theory the better it is. That's my theory. And very good I've found it."

Boyd shook his head. "Me, I've always been prodigal," he said.

"Well, young fella, you can't expect the Chief to kill any fatted calves for you." Harper chortled hoarsely.

Boyd accepted the thrust with good nature. "Where does this fit in your principle of parsimony ?" he asked, producing a piece of paper from his notebook.

"Let's see it.   Yes, that's the letter he was writing."

He examined it carefully.

"It's my opinion," he said judicially, "that this was done on purpose. 'Chuck it all.' He probably started to write to Dean explaining his act, and then half way through he decided she didn't give a damn about his being sentimental. 'Always be together.'   Rot.   Write that to Dean ? Ha, ha.

"Then the idea came to him that if he left the letter half finished his wife would get the blame. She being the only one in the house that had reason enough to shoot him.   And he was almost right ! If it was murder, she was it.   What'd you think, Lewis ?"

"It sounds quite reasonable, I think," Lewis replied thoughtfully.   "It's much simpler than it looked at first.   I think your case will hold water anywhere."

"That's right," Harper agreed complacently. "Well, that's it, I guess.   What do you think, Boyd ?"

"Oh, it's all right with me, Inspector," the young man said with a shrug.   "It's plausible enough."

"Well, then, I'll turn in a report on it, eh ?"

He beamed in a conciliatory fashion. "Now, there's another point.

"We'll have to talk it over with the Chief. But I don't think there'll be any trouble about it. There's no getting away from it. Scoville cheated the gallows. He murdered Thomas and the Dean woman as sure's you're born. But hell, they're dead, and no great loss either. Now if we aired all that, a lot of people besides the Chilterns would get splashed. Eh ? I say then, let Thomas and Dean go for the papers to use in the next flurry about the Yard's unsolved murders."

A dry sideways smile lighted his great face for an instant, and he struggled into his overcoat with a throaty submerged chuckle.

"Coming, Boyd ?" he asked. "S' long, Major Lewis."

Mr. Slade padded along after them without a word.

I looked at Lewis, who was smoking as calmly, now the thing was over, as when he began it, his face a genial mask. And then it all dawned on me.

"So *this* is what you've been leading up to ?" I demanded. "You meant suicide the other night, not that Mimi Dean had done it ?"

"Good man, Braithwaite," he said. I think for all his carelessness about such things he was rather pleased at my appreciation of his subtlety.

"Well," he said, "I rather thought Harper would

settle it all in a jiffy. He's shrewd old fellow, and he has a mortal abhorrence — as I dare say you noticed — of the complicated. So there we are, eh ? It's always better to let the police settle these things. It's so much more expeditious and final that way."

"So this is the end ?" I said.

"Ah no. There's the diamond still to be found," he reminded me. I had completely forgot the thing in the exultation of the police's finding. Then I thought of Catherine upstairs.

"Sha'n't we tell Mrs. Scoville ?" I said. I knew what the girl was going through, although fine patrician stock doesn't show such things as ordinary people would.

"Yes, I think so," he said, getting up and knocking out his pipe thoughtfully into the fireplace.

Catherine was in her sitting room, paler than usual, but calm enough. The shining vitality of her chestnut hair with hints of gold shooting unexpectedly through it, was in glorious contrast with the lassitude of her slim body, sunk in a deep chair. The dark weary eyes were even more prominent against the pallor of her face, which was thinner now. Her skin had taken on an almost transparent quality.

"Dr. Norland took my father back to Chiltern," she said listlessly, without taking her eyes away from the fire.

"Catherine !" I said. "The police have found

that Scoville committed suicide." I took her cold hand in mine.

"I know," she replied. "Richard Boyd stopped in to tell me. But what of that?" she cried suddenly, almost hysterically. "Oh, Major Lewis, can't you find the diamond? It will kill my father. His heart won't stand it much longer; he had a bad attack here this morning. He's very ill. I'm almost frantic. You must find the diamond."

Her voice was urgently pleading, although she hadn't moved except to clasp and unclasp her long white hands.

"Mrs. Scoville!" Lewis's voice was curiously gentle, and so were his eyes. "I think Braithwaite knows everything there is to be known, doesn't he — about all this?"

We both looked up, startled, at such an assertion.

"I don't mean the diamond," he added. "I mean everything else. The divorce proceeding, and so on?"

She nodded and raised her eyes to mine. I think I could — well, I was very much affected by what I saw in them. More than I had ever been, I fancy.

"Then, Mrs. Scoville," he said, breaking the spell she had cast over me, "do you still wish to make me believe that Nelson Scoville was not a thief, as well as all the rest?"

She shook her head silently.

"Your husband did steal your diamond, when you caught him at your safe. Later in his rooms, that Monday night, you had words with him. He gave you back the diamond which you sent to your bank. But the diamond was paste. Aren't you convinced of that ?"

She nodded dumbly.

"But other things happened too, that night ? Your husband was not alone. Miss Dean was with him. It was she who gave you the diamond ? Scoville had stolen it for her — in a sense. It was the offering he was making her, in an attempt to get her to stay with him. They told you, just to humiliate you. They made you suffer through your pride, because they knew you'd never tell about it. But when you threatened to shoot, if they didn't give up the stone, they hadn't counted on that ?"

"Yes," she replied quietly. "That's what happened. When I went in she had it on. It made me furious to see our diamond around *her* neck."

"And then, Mrs. Scoville, you told them you were divorcing him. He hadn't got your letter to him in Paris, of course. Did anyone at all know about the divorce, except Braithwaite ?"

"No. Father doesn't believe in divorce."

"Then there is just one thing that I must ask you. What did Scoville tell you then, that made you 'phone to Braithwaite at three o'clock in the morning, to tell him *not* to file your papers the next day ? As you'd directed him to do the day before ?"

She stared at me in horror, and I weakly at Lewis, who said gently, "Calls from Kensington are not common at three o'clock in the morning. That one was very easy to trace. Braithwaite didn't give away the secret. On the contrary, he's been much too secretive."

She cut short my protests. "I should have told you. But I thought . . . oh, well, I thought for a while that perhaps it needn't come out. And Hartwell was in it too, and I couldn't. Monday night, after Miss Dean returned my diamond, they told me that Nelson was not my husband. That he had married her, as Elmer Wilson, in Bristol in 1916. They thought Wilson was killed in the war. They took his name, because she was a dancer, and Lord Scoville would never have allowed the marriage. And all his friends knew she'd been living with this Wilson before.

"They lived together in various places, secretly and openly. But you know all this ?" she asked pathetically.

"I guessed much of it," he replied gently. "The clerk in Bristol has identified Scoville as E. Wilson, and the bank manager where Dean and Wilson had a safe box did the same. Wilson was Nelson Scoville, and he and Dean had their stocks and passports in Wilson's name."

She went on. "Then Wilson turned up just before our marriage. We Chilterns needed money. Thomas had heard about Nelson's former marriage in Bristol, and he attached himself to Nelson as valet. I despised the creature, and tried to get Nelson to get rid of him. But of course he couldn't . . ."

"And then," Lewis went on for her, "Thomas blackmailed both Scoville and Dean until they took him into partnership, as it were. Because your alleged husband, besides being a thief, was also a blackmailer."

Catherine hardly shrunk under this statement. Her pride had suffered too intensely to feel anything more, I think.

"But, unless I'm mistaken, he made a bad mistake: he tried to butter his bread on both sides. Last week, when Scoville and Miss Dean were getting ready to leave the country and be rid of him, he got the wind up and went down to Chiltern."

Only Catherine's widening eyes showed that she had heard him.

"I must admit that for a time I thought you had . . . imagined the barrel-organist you spoke of. But I had the matter looked into. The man whom you saw on the street outside here is one Tony Harvey. He's duly registered and licensed, and has no criminal record. But Tony Harvey says he rented his kit and license to a certain person, who I have no doubt was Thomas. And Thomas, with the kit and license, went down to Chiltern, to see what he could get for the knowledge he had. And at Chiltern the constable on duty saw him, one afternoon, talking to you, Mrs. Scoville, at the Park Lodge."

Catherine, elbows propped on her knees, had sunk her head into her hand. She nodded painfully.

"But I'm not sure what he told you," Lewis added, a little whimsically.

"I thought you knew everything," she replied drily. "He told me my husband had not been in Europe but was living with another woman somewhere. That he was a blackmailer, and was planning to leave the country. He offered to tell me more for a large sum of money. At first I didn't believe him, of course. I thought whatever Nelson had done, he couldn't be so vile as that. But I couldn't stop him, and after I'd thought it over I saw it was true. Then I couldn't bear it any longer. I wrote to the French address he'd left, and told him I was going to divorce him. He would know what evidence I had. Then I called up my friend" — she looked at me — "but we didn't dare tell father."

"Then Thomas," Lewis said, "didn't appear again, because he was dead; and the barrel-organist you saw Monday here was the real one. And on Monday night, when you told Scoville and Miss Dean you were divorcing him, they told you they were already married, and threatened to expose the bigamous relationship unless you withdrew your suit at once."

She nodded again.

"And you yielded to that threat because . . . ?"

"Because of my son," she said quietly. "He would be illegitimate. He couldn't inherit the title."

Lewis nodded, understandingly, looking quietly at her with a curious intentness.

"What shall you do now?" he asked.

"I don't know. I haven't thought about it. It's all so unreal. I can't make myself believe that it's over. That he killed himself, and that Ronnie and I are free again. I'll go to father for a while, then to Spain or somewhere for a rest. Then come back. There's not much else to do."

"But there's a lot else to think," Lewis said. "If I were you I'd tell myself that I played the game as decently as I could, and then forget all about it. You're very young, really, you know."

Her eyes widened as she looked up at him standing very large and capable and kindly in the middle of the room. They looked at each other a long moment, her eyes filling with tears; and then she dropped her head into her hands.

CHAPTER TWENTY-TWO

"WHAT will they do now, the police, I mean?" I asked Lewis as we got our things in the hall.

"They'll wait until the inquest next week, and then the jury will bring in a verdict of suicide while of an unsound mind," he said. "In most cases that's rather hard on the relatives. It implies a strain of insanity in the family. In many cases the suicide may have been the sanest act the person ever performed."

I was a little startled at this hardened attitude from Lewis, but I had to admit it described Scoville's act truly. It was the safest way out, I added.

"Think so?" he remarked with a barely stifled yawn. "Ah well, I dare say you're right. And now, I have some loose ends to tie up, and the diamond."

I was a little reluctant to leave him until I'd seen the very last of this thing. I had pledged myself, of course, to see Catherine through. Not, indeed, that I felt she was any longer in the least danger; but there was little doubt in my mind that this last interview with Lewis had done a great deal to prejudice her in his eyes. That isn't exactly what I mean. But I couldn't get it out of my head that there was still something about Catherine's part in the whole affair that he wasn't completely satisfied with. That feeling will explain my present reluctance to leave the matter.

"It's perfectly ghastly about the Muscovy Diamond," I said tentatively.

He glanced at me, and again that disconcerting twinkle flickered in his eyes an instant.

"Dear me !" he said drolly. "Don't tell me you don't know where the diamond is either ?"

I was dumfounded.

"You don't mean to imply that *I* know anything about the thing !" I was considerably annoyed when he chuckled in great amusement.

"Come, Braithwaite," he said genially. "I know you to be an upright member of the Law. I only thought you'd probably guessed where the diamond is, because I have. We'll let it go at that."

"But my dear sir," I said. "The Chilterns . . ."

"I'm not quite ready to tell them yet," he said quietly. "The diamond is perfectly safe, I think. As a matter of fact, I rather hoped you hadn't guessed where it is. Not a word about this, please."

His voice had a curiously steely quality. "I've put no restrictions on you, Braithwaite, so far; but I'm putting one on now. You're not to let this out till I say you may."

He said it very affably, but glancing at him I knew he meant what he was saying. My mind flew back to the intimate appeal in Catherine's eyes. What did it mean, I thought? What did this man know about the wretched jewel?

I caught an amused glance from him. Then he said more gravely, "You see, Braithwaite, there are still so many things unexplained — or unattached, I think we can explain them well enough — in this case, that I'm giving a few more days to it. I don't want Harper's finding to be upset by lack of positive evidence.

"For instance, the buying of the chocolates. I suppose there's no doubt it was Scoville who gave them to the messenger. A large man, middle-aged — well, Scoville was heavy enough to give that impression in the dark. Clearly it wasn't Maitland-Rice. He's light. And Thomas, I suspect, was dead when they were handed so secretly, on the dark side of Redcliffe Square, to Doolan.

"However, I think there's no reasonable doubt that Thomas bought the things. Boyd has established that pretty well. He may not have known what they were to have been used for; probably didn't. Scoville was in the habit of sending Miss Dean gifts of the kind.

"And then, there's another thing to be explained — where the arsenic came from. They haven't traced the buyer definitely. If you get it in small quantities, it's mixed with indigo or something as a precaution. Now Maitland-Rice is the only person who knew the girl who had the means directly at hand.   He uses the stuff in quantities, of course, for preserving his bird skins.   He has a rather fine collection by the way, at the Norland's place, where he's going to live after his marriage.   We might call on him sometime . . . Well, I'm off to Shepherd's Bush.   So long."

I couldn't think off-hand of any decent enough excuse to go with him.   So I went back to talk to Catherine.

The next few days I spent minding my own business, as Boyd baldly put it, when I suddenly met him in Paradise Court coming out of Simpson's.

The case was to come up before the coroner on Friday noon.   It was Thursday morning, and a week and a day — it seemed a year — since Catherine had frantically summoned me to that grisly scene.   Boyd wasn't sure how many of us would be called.   The Chief was anxious to spare Catherine as much as possible, especially now that she was at Chiltern attending to her father.   He had taken to his bed with a combination of cold, heart, and nerves.   Everyone marvelled that he stood up under it as well as he'd done.   The disappearance of the diamond had leaked out, of course, although we'd made every effort to cover it up.   It was running all over the front pages of the Americanized papers and the middle pages of the papers unsmirched by such overseas methods.   The police were of the opinion that it was not immediately

concerned in the murders.   I had not seen Lewis
for some days.

I was mostly impressed, I think, by Boyd's eager-
ness to acquit Lewis of all blame or share in his ini-
tial mistake.   "I was there first," he said.   "I
should have seen it was a suicide.   Old Horsey
Harper's right about it.   He's·been at the game
long enough not to get carried away by his own
smartness.   When Monk came along I'd messed up
the works.   He didn't have a chance to see how
simple it was."

The inquest appeared to be perfunctory.   The
police brought in their evidence.   The coroner
made some sarcastic remarks about young police de-
tectives — who, he hinted, owed their position to
influence rather than to merit — who confused
crime with jackstraws and saw everything through
eyeglasses chequered like cross-word puzzles.   He
was being pushed just then as a prominent humor-
ous figure, and his jokes were given adequate space
in the papers on the following day, but I saw very
little in them, as a matter of fact.   Boyd retired
with little glory and amidst a certain amount of
good-humored nudging among the jury wiseacres.

I was surprised when Major Gregory Lewis,
D.S.O., was called.   Only his burly presence, which
rather subdued the coroner, I thought, saved him
from treatment similar to Boyd's.

He explained again that Scoville was left-handed

and was believed to have had enemies, and that until it was shown that he customarily shot with his
right hand — the picture from Country Life was
handed to the jury; he had verified the fact from
friends of the dead man — it seemed plain enough
that it was murder.

Who had verified the fact ? the coroner asked.

Lieutenant John Middlemore of the Guards; the
Master of the Borland Hunt; a gardener at Lord
Scoville's estate who had known him from boy-
hood; and his elder brother, Lord Scoville.   Lewis
had investigated it pretty thoroughly.

"You are satisfied then, that it is a case of suicide ?" the coroner asked, shaking his spectacles at
him admonishingly.

Lewis's slow smile seeped though the jury box
and down through the spectators with contagious
good humor.   Even the coroner relaxed the sever-
ity of his squint.

"You stated it pretty plainly in your opening
address, I fancy," he said.   The coroner jotted
down what he remembered of his rebuke to Boyd
to use again or to tell his wife.

Inspector Harper's report was completely accepted.   The unhesitating verdict was suicide
while of unsound mind.   No doubt to the jury the
statement of Scoville's £12,000 liabilities, opposed
to his £22 assets, on top of his wife's suit for divorce, which had to come out in my testimony,
seemed enough cause for insanity to justify or at

any rate to explain, any act of self-destruction.
No doubt they held to the Dickensian budget.
Happiness, one pound income, expenditures something less; misery, one pound income, expenditures
a fraction over.   I forget the exact figures.

Lewis went away without more than a perfunctory nod to me across the heads of the crowd of reporters and curious public that makes up the little
world before which the coroner struts and plays
the wit or the moralist according to his humor.   I
saw him talking to Boyd in the corner, but he got
away before I could catch him.

After dinner that evening I couldn't resist the
temptation of dropping around to see Lewis in
Bedford Square.   There was something about the
man that attracted me very much, but which I
tried in vain to analyse.   Whether it was his
rugged, pleasant, and very dependable-looking
face, or the eyes, kindly but too steady to be as gentle and harmless as they seemed, I don't know.   I
felt, at any rate, almost as if it was impossible for
me to stay away.

He was going over a pass-book, and I suddenly
realized with dismay that we hadn't paid him.   I
muttered something of the sort.

"Oh, these aren't mine."   He seemed amused at
the idea.   I then noticed that he had several of
them.

"They belong to Mimi Dean, Nelson Scoville,
Elmer Wilson *qua* Wilson and *qua* Thomas; Nel-

son Scoville *qua* Elmer Wilson and *qua* Talbot;
and Lord Chiltern and Catherine Chiltern." He
spread them over the table with a chuckle.

I made some gesture of surprise.

"You'll remember that Boyd advised you to
watch your pass-book, Braithwaite. He's quite
right. And, of course, if you've a number of pass-
books in a number of names, then you've got to
watch them all. It eventually becomes quite complicated.

"Scoville, for instance, had these three. Here
he is as Nelson Scoville, here as Wilson, here as Talbot. The writing is disguised in the second and
third, but they're the same, and they agree basically
with the signature on the Bristol register where he
married Mimi. Elmer Wilson — or Thomas —
has a totally different hand, and it checks with the
signatures of him that they have at the various in-
stitutions he graced at one time or another.

"Mimi's writing is straightforward enough, both
as that of herself and as Mamie Wilson. So are
the two Chilterns, of course. Well, it's an interesting study. I've enjoyed the case very much.
I mean professionally speaking. I don't think I
ever went quite so far afield before — or so far as I
nearly did."

He grinned boyishly at me. "One must do
one'self justice, after all, Braithwaite."

"What's it all about now ?" I asked presently.

"Not just sure myself. Perhaps you can help me. Don't be alarmed — but I fancy there aren't a great many of their legal secrets left in your hamper."

I acknowledged the truth of that.

"I understand," he went on, "that until Catherine's marriage the Chilterns were pretty hard up. Right ?"

I nodded. "That's common knowledge," I admitted.

"Chiltern Hall was badly run down ?"

I corrected that. "They'd been making repairs for several years."

"But not very extensively."

I admitted they were rather minor, in view of the condition of the place.

"Then when did the major repairs begin ? I mean the restoring of the house and park. I understand both are in fairly good condition now."

Although I did not understand what he was getting at, an icy hand laid itself on my heart. I wished to God I had never met this man. His face was still genial and smiling, but the little wrinkles held no trace of amusement, nor could I mistake the steely light in the friendly eyes.

"A year or so after Catherine's marriage," I answered as placidly as I could.

"But Mrs. Scoville has never had much money from that marriage," he returned quietly.

"You forget that she had £2000 a year, and that that seemed a fortune to a girl who'd never had more than £200."

"True enough," he said thoughtfully. "And of course, she did help her father. That's all in these little volumes here. Mrs. Scoville is admirably methodical, and also an excellent manager. She's given her father £500 a year, a quarter of her income, since her marriage. With the rest she's kept up a fairly expensive establishment and passed for a wealthy woman.

"On the other hand, Lord Chiltern's own income is very little, probably not enough to run the place, as he's running it now; and the repairs to Chiltern Hall have cost at least twice five hundred a year. And he has a balance in the bank."

"My dear sir," I said, most acutely dismayed, "what *are* you getting at?"

"Oh, nothing in particular," he replied, with an attempt at lightness. "I'm interested in the Muscovy Diamond, that's all. These little books tell an interesting story. Wilson, Thomas, Dean, Scoville, Talbot, Scoville-Wilson; blackmail, theft, suicide, murder; Lord Chiltern's expensive living, costly repairs, disappearing diamonds, paste replicas. Complicated, isn't it? It's a complete lesson in how to stretch your income. Have a drink, Braithwaite!"

CHAPTER TWENTY-THREE

I THINK I must have become a little intoxicated that night. Everything is very hazy. I know I walked miles before I turned in at Hans Crescent. I must have wandered down Knightsbridge instinctively. I remember staring vacantly at Harrod's window on the corner for I don't know how long. I was barely conscious of the figure that looked like a great bat that kept bearing down on me and then disappearing. A loud cough roused me to the recognition that it was a constable in his rubber cape, that it was raining, and that I'd better get along.

It's not too much to say that I was literally stunned by all this. When I thought it over the implications were too plain. Catherine, lovely Catherine Chiltern — was she a rose cankered at the heart ? For almost six years she had lived with a man like Scoville. Had she waited that time, until a fortune was within his reach, to divorce him; to have her subtle revenge ?

And the diamond. Even Lewis, who had seen her twice, had wondered why so proud a woman would tie herself to such a creature. Or was the diamond the answer ? She had sold it — the Chiltern diamond, the present of royalty — and she had waited six years because she would need all the Scoville fortune to conceal her theft.

Then at the last she had accused Scoville and the Dean woman, when they were dead, of stealing it and substituting for it a piece of worthless paste. I couldn't reconcile such treachery with Catherine. But the Chilterns had been wild in their youth. What if Chiltern strength had turned back to cunning ? She had lied to me and to her father; there was excuse for that; but a Chiltern who could bring herself to sell the Muscovy Diamond would stick at nothing. And her father ! Was she watching him now, slowly dying perhaps, waiting, hoping he would pass away before he could learn of her wanton treachery, got from her French mother ?

For a moment I could not think; and then slowly another and more terrible idea dawned upon me. Her father; Lord Chiltern ! It was he who had repaired Chiltern Hall, he who had somewhere found the money for it. Had he at last sold the diamond; was he in deathly fear lest the truth come out ? That was more than I could comprehend. A woman has no honor — she fights with whatever comes to hand. But a man cannot. I had loved and honored Lord Chiltern for twenty years and more. Could he betray the honor of generations of his family while he pretended to hold it so proudly ?

I was in my rooms before my fire, a picture of Catherine on the mantel, and the tears were streaming down my face. I made no attempt to check them. It was not I who was crying. I was calmly reviewing the years that had passed since I had known and loved the Chilterns. I lived through each little incident, far from my chair before the fire, with Catherine's picture on the mantel. I think I fell asleep sitting there.

My man woke me up with studied disapproval on his face. Surveying the wreck of my shirt front, I found curiously enough that in some way I was immensely refreshed. The events of the evening before marched decently across my mind, the hideousness of evil gone from them all. Whatever happened, I knew clearly what my future attitude towards the Chilterns would be.

I finished my bath and breakfast so decorously, and so free from the nervousness that had depressed me since Catherine called me from my kippers, that my man had only the evidence of my shirt-front to support the conclusion he had plainly arrived at.

I was going with Lewis to Chiltern Hall on the 10:40. It was all very clear to me, and in the taxi I broke into uncontrollable laughter at the whole thing. My conduct so surprised me that I began seriously to take stock of myself, and gradually recovered my usual gravity, which remained nevertheless shot through with a buoyance that I was at a loss to account for.

Lewis was much the same as usual. I suppose

I'd expected him to change overnight too. But he hadn't, not even his rough tweeds and brown boots. He scrutinized me mildly and I bore up under it with amazing imperturbability.

"I've been making a few more investigations, during the past days," he said, when we were settled in our places and rushing towards the South Downs. "I was going to tell you about them last night when you barged out like a lunatic. I hope you got home all right," he added.

"In the last week, since the inquest, I've been to Bristol, Shepherd's Bush, Whitechapel, Park Lane, Camberwell, Moreton Gardens, and Chiltern Hall. Not to mention the Rectory nearby.

"I've interviewed Maitland-Rice both here and at the Rectory, Hicks, Flora, the sweet-shop girl, Davidson, Potts the taxi-man, Mrs. Maxwell, bank clerks and managers, Doolan and what not. In fact, I've had a most depressing time."

"Ah ?" I said politely. "And why are we going to Chiltern again ?"

"Well, I've some information for them. And I thought you might like to visit Miss Margaret Norland and the rector. I have a great fancy, myself, for delicate ladies."

"Spirituelle-like ?" I inquired, quoting Boyd.

He smiled. "Did you read the rector's sermon in one of the Sunday papers ? 'The Devil moveth around like a roaring lion, seeking whom he may devour.' He referred to modern evils, including actresses. I don't think he would have liked Mimi Dean, so we can be pretty sure he didn't send her presents. Although he's a very large man, and he looks much younger than he is."

"What did you find out, on your Cook's Tour?" I asked, as casually as I could.

"Lots of things, and nothing," he said. This lucidity failed to clear much up. "It's mostly been a succession of life histories, interesting sociologically rather than artistically. Like one or two of them?

"Elmer Wilson went to Borstal when he was eleven. He was trained to be an electrician. He had quick hands and a fair head, but there was a quirk in the moral make-up somewhere. No doubt that could be accounted for by his parents, if one of them hadn't been hanged and the other wasn't unaccountably missing. Elmer Wilson could do all sorts of things with his hands, I've learned. He could carve, mend clocks and the like. Typewrite, too, and he was a fairly good plumber. They have a very complete record of his attainments at Borstal, and at Pentonville too, and very interesting I found them. He did expert stone-cutting of a sort, among other things. So expert in fact that he and a couple of others nearly escaped.

"But Elmer Wilson was a coward. He was sent off to the front one fine day, and he cleverly changed identification disks with a poor devil who

was killed. He sneaked out, and he wasn't caught.
Lloyd Thomas, deserted while in action, was hunted
a while, but he didn't turn up, except later as John
Thomas, at Moreton Gardens in 1923.

"His friends in Camberwell and elsewhere knew
him as a shrewd, shifty, and crooked one with a patron who kept him in funds. That's all about
Elmer.

"Then Mr. Maitland-Rice. He interests me, as
a character, I mean. He has no vices, like poor
Elmer Wilson. He's a gentleman, brought up,
much to his detriment in some ways, in the swells
of a strong-minded woman. You'll remember
Boyd says Miss Norland was something like Maitland-Rice's mamma. Well, so far as I can see,
physically she's nothing on earth like her. So I
assume she's like her in mind and soul. Delicate
strong-minded women, Braithwaite, are to be
feared like the wrath of God. I don't envy Maitland-Rice, I must say; unless he actually needs
something made in his mother's image."

"What will happen when she finds out about
Mimi Dean and . . . ?"

"And the letters, and the arsenic?" Lewis finished as I hesitated. A slow smile dawned and
faded. "I think he's told her. Or somebody has.
I swear she knows all about it, though she denied
it firmly. But it won't make any difference.
She's decided to marry him — though I can't just

see why — and she'll do it . . . and I don't think anybody'll stop her."

We relapsed into silence until we drew into Horsham, where we got out and found a car to finish our trip. We figured the fast train and car got us there quicker than the train that stopped at the village, although I don't suppose actually we saved more than half an hour.

I was surprised at Lewis's luggage. Besides his suitcase he had a very bulky package that he carried himself. I had noticed it on the seat beside him in the train. He held it on his knees in the car, and offered no explanation, although my curiosity must, as usual, have been very obvious.

Chiltern Hall and Chiltern Park stretched beautifully before us as we drove over the brow of a pleasant hill. My heart beat a little quicker, as it has never failed to do since the first morning I stood there more than twenty years ago, my green felt brief bag under my arm, before I descended the slope to the tangled jungle that was then Chiltern. I looked back on it now, and it seemed the most important single step I'd ever taken. The Chilterns had figuratively never let me out of their jungle, though it had now become a smiling park, blooming with late chrysanthemums and shiny with red-flecked holly trees and well-trimmed box.

Catherine, still very pale but strangely vital, met us at the door.

"My father is better today, Major Lewis," she said, extending her hand. "Hartwell Davidson is here. I hope you don't mind that? He has a right to know everything."

We followed her into the large library that extends half the length of the main wing. Davidson shook hands with us, and Lord Chiltern, very haggard and very old, raised his hand in silent greeting. He was very ill, I could see, and as I'd never seen him ill in all the years I'd known him, the shock was greater.

Catherine and her father seemed to be curiously quiescent, as though prepared for almost anything. Even at that, they rose splendidly above the sharp anxiety that haunted the dark eyes of young Davidson. He moved restlessly about the room, his hands twitching nervously in the pockets of his flannel jacket.

"I've come for two reasons." Major Lewis seemed quite naturally the one of us to speak. "They aren't particularly connected, although one couldn't have happened without the other. What I mean is that either wouldn't have happened if the other hadn't, although either, probably, would have been followed by the other."

He smiled, and added, "Maybe that isn't very clear. But let's leave it at that."

Davidson hadn't taken his eyes off Lewis since he came in. The expression in them was that of a man who had been through hell and had stumbled just as he reached sight of paradise. My gaze turned involuntarily to Catherine. I couldn't believe treachery or faithlessness of any sort lurked in her eyes. There were no shadows in which they could hide.

"The first is probably the more important, from one point of view," Lewis was saying gently; "that of Society. You all know, I think, that Nelson Scoville didn't commit suicide. He was murdered."

No sound broke the silence of the room. Lewis was filling his pipe slowly and methodically. He hadn't looked at anyone. I was watching him, and he went on without more than casually meeting our eyes.

"You knew that, Mrs. Scoville?" he asked, as placidly as if he were asking if she knew the sun shone on Chiltern Rill.

"I knew it," she said. Her voice was low and vibrant. "I knew it, because . . . because I knew he'd never take his own life. I knew that from all the terrible things he said on Monday night."

She hesitated a brief space.

"And . . . the window in the library was open when I went downstairs."

A sharp catching of breath was the only sound we heard. Lewis was unscrewing the end of his pipe.

"You remember," she went on more quickly, "when you went upstairs I must have said something; anyway, you came back into the library, just before I closed the window."

"You wanted to protect someone, whom you thought had gone out that way?" Lewis asked, a little tritely.

A faint warmth stole from her throat and flushed her cheeks. She nodded.

"You're quite right," Lewis said, rather abruptly. "Scoville didn't kill himself. Nor did he kill Mimi Dean."

Her eyes were wide and panic-stricken.

"Mimi Dean was poisoned by the same person who killed Nelson Scoville," Lewis went on quietly. "The letter he wrote her was quite genuine. They would be together, and she wouldn't mind very much, because their game was up. Maitland-Rice knew about it, you know about it; Thomas has told you.

"Worse than that, Margaret Norland and her father knew about it. Thomas had told them on the same day that he saw you. He was doggedly trying to collect money, this time from the rector, to save his daughter. Thomas knew Mimi's game and if he didn't have the letters, he knew what was in them. He put the same value on keeping silent that Maitland-Rice did, because, in different ways, they were both cowards.

"But Thomas picked the wrong people. Maitland-Rice couldn't believe that his offence wasn't enough to make a pariah of him — couldn't believe

that, after all, it was a very little sin as sins go these
days. But the Norlands — especially Dr. Norland, as you very kindly pointed out to me one day,
Braithwaite — are made of sterner stuff than Maitland-Rice, or Thomas, or Scoville. Dr. Norland
particularly is emphatically a man of the world.
He was not to be blackmailed. He had the whole
business out of Thomas in five minutes; and he
wrote to Scoville telling him that he intended to
expose him. It was then that they shot and killed
Thomas, under whose real name they planned to
leave England for America.

"What follows is guess-work, but I think there's
not much doubt of it. They planned to move
Thomas's body to Moreton Gardens. What in-
famy they planned there I have no clear idea of,
and it's not very pleasant to go into. It was
diabolical and cunning, enough so that Mrs. Scoville perhaps would not have survived it."

He stopped and filled his pipe with extraordinary
care and deliberation.

"By the way," he continued, as if he were about
to discuss a new play, "perhaps you don't all know
that Lord Scoville, the old lord I mean, was a very
simple old man with a thousand and one theories
that he loved to put into practice. The present
lord gave me the manuscript of a book he was writing on the subject of Heredity *versus* Education,
His contention in it is that heredity is complete
rubbish, and that environment is solely responsible

for what a person becomes. To prove it, he adopted six boys. His nephew, the present lord — who happened to be his heir also — and five others, selected at random from different strata of society. None of the six was his son at all. He was completely celibate all his life. He took each of the children before it was two days old, and placed it in what he considered an ideal environment — his own home.

"Well, each child had everything that refinement and culture and the intelligent use of great wealth can give. Each was totally ignorant of his or the others' origin, and each believed that Lady Scoville was his mother and Lord Scoville his father. Lady Scoville died, eventually, with a broken heart and sealed lips.

"And all the boys turned out well, except one. That was Nelson Scoville. The old lord was convinced then that Nelson only needed longer treatment than the others, and he felt that if married to a good woman he would eventually prove the theory.

"Catherine Chiltern was his ideal woman. He believed that if Nelson married her, he would buck up and be like his alleged brothers. He decided then to leave Nelson's share of the property to him only if that did happen. He left the money, as we all know, in Mrs. Scoville's hands. If things went well, Nelson would get a share of the money; if not, it remained, as a sort of recompense, to Mrs. Scoville."

Catherine's face was as white as death, her eyes great burning pools. No sound came from her frozen lips. These facts, so simply stated, beat in upon each of us with varying terrible implications.

"Rather a cross for a woman to bear," Lewis was saying casually. "Lord Scoville believed in crosses. He was a friend of Ruskin, in his youth. He also thought it proper that women should bear them. He seems to have believed in a curious atonement — each woman for each man. He only started his book. He was too honest to go on with it when he found Nelson upsetting his theory. He left it then, with great simplicity and purity of intention, for the present lord to finish — after Mrs. Scoville had succeeded in completely establishing the thesis. It's a very interesting book — although his heir hasn't ventured to add anything to it — and he was a very interesting old chap."

God knows none of us could think of him as anything but a monstrous old man whose shadow lay over us like a pall.

Lord Chiltern's head was sunk on his breast. They say a drowning man sees his whole life in a flash before him. Lord Chiltern was drowning in a bitter sea. What would his heir, Nelson Scoville's son, be ?

"Well, Scoville found out very quickly and decidedly from Dr.. Norland that Thomas had betrayed them. He knew he hadn't time to carry out the plan, which I have no doubt in the world he had formed, to incriminate Mrs. Scoville as the slayer of Thomas. He knew the game was up, and that he and Mimi had no time to waste. He knew it better than she did, because he was more cautious and more cunning.

"They needed all the money they could get. And here the Chiltern diamond comes in. They had always planned, I fancy, to get it. Why they hadn't tried before I don't know. Perhaps they had," he added, as he saw a faint flush mount to Catherine's ivory throat. "Scoville then stole it, Monday night, after bargaining all day with your friend Lennert, Davidson. Lennert took twenty-four hours to decide to give up the deal, not three; and I think then it was necessity that made him decide so.

"Mrs. Scoville caught them, and acted precisely as they knew she would do, and as they wished her to do. They returned the diamond; but the diamond they returned was, as we know, paste."

His level gaze fastened itself evenly on Lord Chiltern, and stayed a moment before turning on Catherine.

"Scoville wanted you to know, you see, that he had taken the diamond, and he wanted you to see it on the woman who was his legal wife. He let her give it back to you, because in that way he was being more subtle.

"He had counted, and correctly, on the Chiltern pride. He had lost the opportunity to ruin your life by his first plan, but he could hurt you cruelly by his second. Because Mimi Dean had the Muscovy Diamond. She calmly put it in her pocket, walked out of the house before your very eyes, past the men whom the alarm had brought, stepped into her car and drove to Park Lane.

"Tuesday she refused to see Scoville because she thought the less they were together just then the better. There was no quarrel. Wednesday she rang up, and I answered the 'phone. She didn't know that he was dead, and she asked flippantly if it was Shepherd's Bush 6408. While I hesitated, she asked Scoville to come to the club that evening. I knew who it was then, and told her that Mr. Scoville could not answer the telephone. She saw something was wrong and hung up. I got a man to follow her at once. Luckily he got to Park Lane just as she was leaving. He lost her in a big store in Knightsbridge, picked her up later, and followed her home.

"When we searched her house a little later, the diamond, which even then I was sure she had taken, was not there. Nor has it been seen since."

He picked up the parcel he'd brought from town and guarded so carefully, while we watched in silence. He tore off the wrappings, and held up a long, wonderfully soft, grey squirrel coat.

"All grey fur coats are the same to my man Tate," he said with a whimsical smile. "Mimi Dean walked straight to the fur cold storage department, when she had lost Tate in that store, and put away her squirrel coat until she should call for it. And she bought an imitation one for fourteen guineas and wore it out."

As he was speaking he put his hand in each pocket in turn, and at last, from a tiny pocket in the cuff of the left sleeve, he drew out a dainty wad of handkerchief and spread it open on the table. On its silken surface burned and gleamed the Muscovy Diamond.

CHAPTER TWENTY-FOUR

AFTER luncheon I talked with Lord Chiltern a little. Now that the diamond was safely back, nothing appeared to matter very much to him.

While we were having coffee after luncheon Ronald's nurse brought him in. He was very like Catherine, I thought — I'd not seen him for some months — except that he was a sturdy robust little fellow. His eyes sparkled and his cheeks were rosy red from a vigorous life in the country air.

"Oh I say, mother, is he here ?" he whispered loudly. "Will he tell me a story about the war ?"

In that house of tragedy the child had walked untouched. I shuddered as I thought what potentialities lay behind red cheeks and merry eyes if old Scoville was wrong and heredity counted, after all. What could a child hope to be, whose father was a cunning scoundrel, a blackmailer, a thief, and a murderer ? In what dark hours would his evil ancestors creep into his soul and lead him to follow their tortuous paths ?

"Mother !" he whispered urgently. "Can I show him my fort ?"

His mother smiled at Major Lewis.

"You see, your fame is before you. Richard Boyd has told my son all about you." But Ronald cared for none of the usual formalities, and very

shortly a big man and a small boy went out together, a small brown hand confidently in a great
brown paw. Lord Chiltern's troubled eyes followed the blithe figure of his little heir. What
doubts and questionings and bitter pain tormented
the old man who had never had a son ? His love
for the child was greater even, I think, than his love
for his daughter.

She was standing by the window with Davidson.
They also were watching the two figures moving
across the lawn to the small plot beyond the Dutch
garden that was the boy's own. It served as battle-
field, airdrome, sea and channel, castle and hunt,
in turn. The first genuinely happy smile I'd seen
for many months broke out on his mother's face.
God knows what she found to smile at, I thought.
I seemed to see a great vulture hovering over the
unconscious child, blotting the sunshine from his
radiant figure. And none of us could stay the
creature — such is the power of heredity. The
evil that men do lives after them, in their children;
it drags them down to the depths.

Catherine was smiling, serenely oblivious. I saw
her hand clasped tightly in the protective grip of
Hartwell Davidson. On his face there was no
happy smile, only bitterness and pain.

After a while Lord Chiltern and I strolled down
to rescue Lewis. "The child will drive him mad,"
he fumed.

I think I could understand his irritation — I

might quite truthfully say, jealousy. The child
was, after all, his chief interest, in a world so far
removed from the bustle and excitement of life.
It was natural that he should be slightly piqued at
the boy's sudden attachment to Lewis. Children
know no half-measures. The youngster hadn't so
much as noticed the rest of us in his delight. Even
now we found him reluctant to part with his new
friend, and only a satisfactory bedtime arrangement induced him to dance off with his grandfather, to conquer new worlds before tea-time.

"Am I presentable, Braithwaite, if we should
happen to meet the Norlands ? But never mind,"
he added, brushing off his knees, "you're sufficiently
immaculate for both of us. Let's chance it."

He removed some of Ronald's trenches from his
heavy boots, and we set out across the park.

He absentmindedly lopped the tops off the grass
with his stick as we took the short cut through the
copse to Norland Abbots. He said nothing even
when we let ourselves through the wicket into the
Norlands' grounds.

"Are they expecting us ?" I asked, not knowing what his intentions were.

"I hope not," he said cheerfully. "There's just
a little matter I'd like to clear up before we an-
nounce ourselves. If you'll make yourself as little
obtrusive as possible, and keep a sharp eye in that
direction, it won't take long."

We made our way quietly through the trees away

from the house. I was surprised that Lewis knew his way about very well. I hadn't supposed his previous visit was so thorough.

"Don't wade through those leaves like a school-boy, Braithwaite," he said under his breath. "The Norlands aren't people who'd be polite to tres-passers. This way."

We came out of the fringe of trees to a small lodge. It was screened from the great house whose chimneys we could see by a dense wood. The place was obviously unoccupied, but Lewis rapped vigorously with the knocker and waited, then knocked again. No one came.

He glanced up at the windows and then behind us, and took a key from his pocket, which he in-serted quickly and noiselessly into the lock. I fol-lowed him into the house with extreme reluctance, yet I don't think it ever occurred to me not to do so.

The hall was perfectly bare except for an old Windsor chair and a table. Lewis opened the door at the right and closed it silently. So also at the left. He listened carefully, then we climbed the stairs. He opened a door at the end of the small corridor and gave a low exclamation of satisfaction. I followed him into the room.

It was a large light apartment with a laboratory table and bench at one end. The walls were lined with closed cabinets, on top of some of which stood glass cases enclosing stuffed and mounted birds.

Lewis opened one of the cabinets. It contained twenty or so trays, each one filled with rows of stuffed birds, neatly labelled and arranged. He closed it and went up to the work table. Here were scissors of various shapes, other implements strange to me, needles, thread, cotton, all neatly arranged in trays by some careful hand. At one side was a box labelled "Poison."

"Very meticulous indeed," Lewis murmured approvingly. He opened the box and put a little of the crystalline white powder in it to his tongue. He spat it out with a wry mouth.

"Are these things Dr. Norland's ?" I whispered.

"They're Maitland-Rice's. He moved his collection and workshop down here a month or so ago. Hello ! What's that ?"

Then my ears also caught the sound of footsteps below.

"Quick, behind the cabinet !" Lewis whispered. "Keep still !"

My heart nearly stopped, then began to beat like a trip-hammer as I squeezed against the wall as silently as I could.

Two voices, muffled, then louder, then very clear, told us the progress of the newcomers. They had entered the room.

"But good Lord, Davidson," I heard. A gentle voice has a curious quality under stress of emotion.

"Can't you *see* ?" cut in the other gruffly. "I've told you they aren't through. Boyd was pulling our leg. Lewis is down here now. He knows something, Lord knows what. Ronald's been telling him about your 'City of Dead Birds' and is going to bring him over after tea. If he finds all this stuff lying about he's going to be suspicious of somebody around here. You've got a whole keg of arsenic. Don't you see?"

"But look here. If he sees me taking it away . . . I think I'd rather leave it." Maitland-Rice could be stiff-necked when he chose. His voice showed an acute anxiety.

"Then I'll do it," said Davidson. "I don't give a damn if he sees me."

We could hear them moving the paraphernalia on the table.

"There's more in the store-room downstairs," Maitland-Rice said as they went quietly out.

In spite of the fact that I was deucedly cramped, and Lewis must have been more so because of his size, we made no move. I waited for him; he stayed stock still until we heard the downstairs door shut.

We slipped out into the room. The poison box was gone, and in its place was a tray of scissors.

"They even remembered to brush off the dust, so it wouldn't look as if anything had been moved," Lewis remarked. "Too bad Mimi wasn't as thoughtful. I wonder which one thought of it?"

He gave me a quizzical look, which instantly became alert.

"Behind again!" he whispered, and we jumped back to our hiding places.

This time it was a single step that we could faintly hear on the uncarpeted stairway. The door opened and hurried steps crossed the room to the table.

We heard a sharp intake of breath and a curious clucking of surprise, tinged, I thought, with alarm. The footsteps retraced themselves.

Lewis sprang lightly from his place as we heard the downstairs door close. We knelt by the window and peered out. No one was in sight but the rector of Chiltern. Dr. Norland was pacing quietly across his domain, engrossed in his breviary.

We let ourselves out the back door of the lodge. My repugnance for creeping in and out of people's houses, spying on them and what not, was heightened by my clear knowledge of the legal seriousness of our offence. Also, I knew Dr. Norland.

"We'll dispense with the rector's company for the time being," Lewis announced, heading through the trees back towards Chiltern Hall. We went in silence for a time. Then he broke into a subterranean chuckle.

"I wonder what he'll do with it?" he said.

"Who?" I asked. "With what?"

"Davidson with the arsenic. It's not so easy to get rid of at a moment's notice. Especially when there's ten pounds or so of it."

"He can bury it," I said feebly.

"And have the undergardener see him, or some dog dig it up in place of his bone ?"

"He could hide it in the garage, then."

"Which is exactly where he'd think I'd look first for it. No, it's harder to get rid of guilty objects than anything in the world, for the simple reason that they are guilty. You know it, and you feel it must be apparent to everybody. So nine times out of ten you avoid the simplest and best things to do. That's where most criminals go wrong. They don't know enough to do the simplest thing, and they don't know when to let well enough alone. That's why police officers are successful in so many cases. They sit about, looking wise, until their man begins to get nervous, or remembers something he forgot, or thinks of something a little cleverer that he hadn't thought of earlier. He multiplies the evidence, if he's trying to implicate some one, or he removes it if he's trying to protect himself."

"Then," I said, "you think Maitland-Rice was right about not wanting to move the arsenic ?"

"Surely. It was madness to do so. It belongs on the ornithologist's worktable. Its being there is no evidence of guilt or guilty intent. Its not being there is in itself suspicious. Its being tucked away in the Chiltern jam-closet is the very clearest evidence that somebody isn't sleeping well o' nights.

"I must say," he added thoughtfully, "that there's been very little last minute work in this case. That's why we've not got on faster. Who-

ever did this job did it well and let it go at that.
He knew when to stop and he hasn't made a move
since. His sole mistake — or almost the sole
mistake — was in connection with this arsenic."

"What do you mean ?" I exclaimed.

"Don't be alarmed. I've known for some time
who did it. The processes of elimination, you
know. Well, I can't prove it now, but I think I
know now that all the others didn't."

In spite of his last remarks I was strengthened in
my determination to find Davidson and tell him to
be careful. What if he were caught red-handed,
so to speak, trying to conceal the arsenic ? In a
case of the sort, motive, combined with circumstantial evidence, has convicted many a man. Any
one who had seen him and Catherine together a few
hours before could hardly doubt that he had motive
to do far more.

Lewis must have felt what was in my mind. He
suddenly began to talk about everything under the
sun: flowers, trees, grass, land-tax and death duties,
and to move with the most maddening deliberation.
He even affected interest in a litter of police pups
that Ronald had told him about, and dragged me a
quarter of a mile out of our way to visit them in the
kennels.

The clock on the stable struck half-past four
before he would hear of our returning to the house,
and all through tea he interrupted every glance of
warning I tried to give Davidson. Davidson in

any case, was completely engrossed in Catherine. His eyes were never off her face. He clearly, I thought, had had a load taken off his mind. He was much more natural than he had been before, and his eyes had a calm determined light in them as he discussed various problems of African development with Lewis, Lord Chiltern, and a local squire who had dropped in.

It was a little after six when Ronald's nurse came in and spoke to Catherine.

"Major Lewis," Catherine said with a smile, "have you forgot your appointment in the nursery ?"

He returned her smile. "I was to be sent for properly," he said.

Catherine and Davidson followed him out of the room, leaving Chiltern, his guest, and myself to carry on. It was my chance to get in touch with Davidson before it was too late, but I couldn't break away. The discussion was on some land-tax or other, and since they were asking my legal opinion I couldn't very well get up and leave, as I strongly wished to do.

The squire finally took his departure, and I rushed out to find Davidson. He wasn't downstairs. His clothes were laid out on his bed, ready for dinner, so I knew he hadn't been there. I thought then I'd better see if Lewis was still safely in the nursery. I went quietly up to the second floor, where my own room and the nursery were. I could always be going in to dress if Lewis saw me. The nursery consists of three rooms; I knew the nurse would not be there, as Catherine always spends the bedtime hour with the child when she is at Chiltern, and so I walked through to the play-room, opened the door quietly and stepped inside. What I heard froze me in my tracks, my hand still on the door. I could neither go back nor speak to let them know I was there. What I heard was never meant for my ears, but I was powerless to stir.

Lewis was speaking.

"You did not sleep in your bed Tuesday night. The maid had put fresh sheets on it that morning. They had been crumpled, but not slept in. She makes endless beds a day and is not deceived so easily. Where did you go after Sanderson left you at one o'clock ?"

"I can't tell you that," I heard Davidson say.

"Didn't you go back to Moreton Gardens ? I think I can tell you your reason for going back there. That afternoon you saw Mrs. Scoville at a friend's home. It was the first time for six years. She told you what her life had been. More than that, she told you why she had married Scoville."

I could hear a faint gasp from Catherine. I could sense the drama those three were playing, their voices tense with emotion, while near them lay the child, wrapped in innocent slumber. The silence for a moment was maddening.

"She married Scoville to conceal your child, Ronald. He is your own son, not Scoville's. And when you learned that, with all the rest of it, you were almost mad with grief and rage."

Davidson's voice answered, almost sobbing. "She told me that afternoon. I wanted to kill the swine. I wanted to tell him the whole thing that night. But I dared not, for Catherine's sake."

With a superhuman effort, I pulled myself together and stepped silently back into the hall. My head was swimming unsteadily. Ronald was Davidson's child. That explained Catherine's sudden capitulation after she had resolutely refused for over a year to marry Scoville. It all came rushing back to me. Davidson had gone to Africa the week before. I knew from a friend that he had gone out to make money, and that Catherine was going to wait for him. There was no breath of scandal when Ronald was born. No one could remotely attach dishonor of any sort to Catherine Chiltern.

Victorian though I may be, I thanked God that all this was true. That Ronald's father was an honest man, whose fault had been — well, who can say? I, for one, am willing to believe it an honest fault. I would condone far greater wrongs to save that innocent child from the pitchy wings of the vampire of heredity that would have folded over his young life had that other been his father.

I went to my room to think it out. I could condone far greater crimes. Lewis could too, I had no doubt. He is a sensible man, and he knew even more of the vileness of Scoville and his friends than I did. But what could Lewis do if he thought that the sin were greater ? What would he say if it were the crime of murder ?

And Lord Chiltern, who doesn't believe in divorce. Had Catherine told him ? I knew he had not known it a week before. He was more Victorian than I myself. I dreaded the effect on him. He had already aged ten years in the last week. The affair of the diamond had nearly been too much for him. Could he bear the truth about his daughter ?

"My daughter, my ducats," began going through my head. That other old man had loved his faithless daughter and his gold. I read his tragedy again in the old peer sitting before the fire downstairs. "My daughter, and my ducats."

The dressing-gong aroused me to activity. Whatever Chiltern might feel, he was old. His daughter was young, Ronald was innocent of any guilt or blame. Davidson and Catherine loved each other, perhaps far more deeply after their years of sadness and separation. Old men have no right to take life from the hands of youth. Above all Catherine and Davidson must not suffer. I tied my tie hurriedly and went downstairs. Lord Chiltern was in his dressing-room.

"I'm glad you've come, Braithwaite," he said. "We have much to talk over."

CHAPTER TWENTY-FIVE

DINNER that evening was the worst ordeal I've ever gone through. Catherine plainly should have been in bed. She sat bravely at the foot of the table, under the suspicious eye of Horace, the ancient butler, before whom it was hopeless to dissemble. Perhaps she had a vision of future peace that held her up. But then I'm sure women are far calmer than men in face of spiritual hardships, perhaps because they are greater materialists than we are.

Lewis was inimitable. He made no effort to be amusing, as many people who knew the situation would have done. He talked gravely and intelligently about many things, America, the Orient, and Africa. He had travelled widely and seen a great deal more than the rest of us. Not once did he allow Catherine to carry the burden of the talk for long, yet I don't think any of us were particularly aware that he had talked almost steadily during the entire meal. I can quite understand why he is in demand among London hostesses of the really discriminating type.

Nevertheless, we were all rather glad to leave the table. With all Lewis's skilled success, I don't think we could have stood it much longer. The atmosphere was too heavily charged to allow normal events to appear satisfactory. The horrid dead faces of Scoville and Mimi Dean and Thomas seemed to close in on us, leering down from the shadowy corners of the great dining hall. I could see their loathsome wild beast's forms, the thin masks of civilization stripped from them, gloating over their victory. They were dead, but they would be avenged. Evil in life, more evil still in death. Theirs would be the victory that makes the fiends in hell laugh.

In the drawing-room we made no effort to talk. We might have been five separate little worlds, each with his own thoughts for a universe, so hedged in by them we were.

Into the silence Horace came, announcing Dr. Norland.

"Take him into the library, Horace," Lord Chiltern said quietly, glancing at Lewis. "You'll excuse us, Kitty." He patted her arm reassuringly. "We'll be back shortly."

I heard Dr. Norland's violent voice. "Damme, Robert ! What's all this nonsense, calling me from my dinner !"

"Nothing much, Eric," Lord Chiltern replied, his hand in his old friend's arm. "You know these people. Give us some whisky, Hartwell, and shut the door."

Dr. Norland I knew was an irascible man. His attitude was bellicose to a degree. He snorted, cocked an angry eye at Lewis, and blew his nose

savagely.   One would never have taken him for a
clergyman except for his collar; but that's often
been said.   Breathing stertorously, he settled himself with his whisky.

Lord Chiltern and I followed suit, while Davidson roamed about the room in the distressing
manner that so many Oxford men have.   Lewis
casually but effectively drew the curtain closely together.   I think he wanted to be sure no one else
had got into the room before he took his place next
to Dr. Norland and filled his pipe.

"You each know part of what I'm going to say,"
he began.   "I don't know how many of you know
it all.

"But I don't want anyone to say anything in the
nature of a confession, for several reasons which
will appear later.   I hope that may be avoided, if
I tell you — the four of you — exactly what happened, and everything that happened, in the case
of Nelson Scoville this last fortnight.

"The police verdict that Scoville killed himself
and the police assumption that it was he who
poisoned Miss Dean, are both wrong.   Their assumption that it was he who killed Elmer Wilson
or Thomas is, I believe, right.

"It is with Thomas that my story begins.   When
he came down here he did not have merely a set of
unsupported assertions about Scoville to sell.   He
had — if this happened as I suppose it to have done,
and I wish anyone would correct me if necessary —

a document, which he left with Dr. Norland. It
is in the form of a confession from Flora Hicks,
Mrs. Scoville's maid. In it she swears that Ronald
Scoville is not the son of his reputed father, but of
Mr. Davidson. It also contains various accusations
against Mrs. Scoville that only a blackguard of the
foulest sort could have imagined. These are not
contained in Flora's statement, but are added to it.
It was a cunning document, for the reason that
Flora knew the truth of the first statement, and
could not truthfully deny it."

Whether this announcement was too incredible
to be believed, or whether each of us had became so
used to devastating truths by this time, I don't
know. A painful silence hung over us like a pall;
each man stared silently in front of him.

"And if she tried to deny it she could be easily
upset," Lewis continued, "not being extremely intelligent. Once the first allegation was proved, the
rest could probably be established, for certain purposes, pretty well by inference. At any rate,
much harm might conceivably be done.

"Scoville had suspected the child was not his
from several things. He told his elder brother so,
a few months after his marriage, and his brother
turned him out of the house. He told me last
week that he had refused to believe or to listen to
such a statement, but that even if it were true, it
did not, of course, affect the legal aspects of his
father's will.

"Scoville had no intention of using that document until the possibly critical time a few months before the will was to be proved. He intended to use it of course only on Mrs. Scoville — he wouldn't dare show it to anyone else — and to compel her to leave him his share of the estate.

"I guessed the truth about the child from what Lord Scoville told me and from his mother's attitude towards him. When I first talked to her, I started to make some harmless comment about the boy; she nearly collapsed to prevent my doing so. I thought then that probably the child was the crux of the matter.

"But all that is over. What remains is the part which the circumstances, the characters and deeds of Scoville and Miss Dean, may justify.

"Mr. Davidson, you left your hotel at about half-past one o'clock on Wednesday morning, and you returned to Moreton Gardens.

"Mr. Braithwaite, you were not in your rooms until half-past two that morning. You don't know the man who lives above you, but he knows you. He heard you come in. In fact, Braithwaite, you're a wolf in sheep's clothing. You misled me every step of the way — or tried to. You withheld the information about the divorce proceedings. You didn't tell me about the telephone call at three o'clock in the morning. You called my attention to the fact that Scoville shot with his right hand. It was you who left the back window

open as you went out of Moreton Gardens at two
o'clock that morning. And it was you who
bought the box of chocolates in the Old Richmond
Road.

"You made several mistakes, Braithwaite. You
badly erred at Moreton Gardens. When you
brushed up the pile of the carpet in Scoville's room,
just before you left, fetching the broom out of the
closet at the end of the hall, you took off your
gloves. You brushed up the carpet, obliterating
all footprints, and you then put the broom back in
the wrong closet and left your finger-prints on the
handle.

"But whatever you did, you did in the train of a
bigger man.

"You didn't shoot Scoville. You wouldn't have
had a chance of coming so close to him, at that time
of night, to fire those shots. Besides, you don't
know how to hold a revolver." He smiled faintly.
"I've seen you handling one.

"No, a large man, one able to cope with Scoville;
who could appear middle-aged in the dark; who
had closer ties at stake, and more personal reasons
to hate or fear Scoville and Mimi Dean than you
had; and who had arsenic at hand to use; that is the
man who shot Scoville, and who sent the chocolates
— which you had innocently got for him — to
Mimi Dean.

"I've thought a good deal about the mind and the
planning of that man," he continued quietly.

"I'm sure he had had a long time to think over the injury they had done him. Indirectly, perhaps, but often the greater for being so. He knew something of the career of those two; how he found it out I don't know. He could not expose them without suffering the consequences. And he knew, also, that Scoville and Miss Dean were preparing to leave the country; or, not knowing or not believing the threatened action for divorce, he only acted in time to prevent Scoville's getting the reward for his six years of good behavior.

"On Monday morning Braithwaite, who was innocent of their intended use, bought a forty-shilling box of chocolates from a shop in South Kensington. I didn't appreciate your annoyance, Braithwaite, at the assistant's unflattering description of the customer, and her unconscious identification of you. And you certainly were not prepared for the scene at Mimi's apartment. It was there that the first glimmerings that you were somehow involved came to me. I must beg your pardon, but for an instant there I thought you might even be one of the girl's lovers.

"You bought the chocolates and gave them to your accomplice. You met him sometime before ten o'clock at Moreton Gardens, when Flora and Hicks were still in the basement. The two of you came openly through the front door of the house and went upstairs to the room opening into Scoville's bathroom. You replaced his box of tooth-powder with one containing arsenic. You then waited in the dark, the two of you, until after midnight you heard Scoville come in. You waited until the house was quiet and you thought he was in bed. You crept through the hall and to the door of his sitting-room. You did not go in. The other man did. He spoke to Scoville, who was sitting at his table writing. When the man spoke, Scoville slipped what he was writing into the first hiding place at hand — the telephone directory by his side. The other man told Scoville what he knew, and raised his revolver. Scoville drew his own from his pocket; but he never fired it. He was shot twice, with an unerring aim, before he could pull the trigger. His own revolver slipped out of his hand onto the table in front of him, and was left there untouched. The shots from Scoville's gun were not fired that night. They were fired the day before; they were the shots that killed Thomas in the Shepherd's Bush house.

"But the revolver was the same calibre as that used to kill Scoville. That had been carefully planned, by someone who knew his possessions well. That there were two shots fired from it was simply luck. His assailant was prepared to leave the revolver he had left; having examined Scoville's, with gloved hands, he saw he had no need to."

There was not a sound while Lewis paused to light his pipe.

"The two of you returned quickly to the room

opening from Scoville's bath. No alarm was raised. Then Braithwaite took the broom from a closet at the end of the hall; or probably had it ready in your room. You carefully swept the rug, and replaced the broom in the linen closet — a bad mistake. While there you disconnected the circuit of the burglar alarms.

"You then went downstairs and out the French window, which you neglected to close securely. That I didn't know until this morning. If I had known it, I should probably have told Harper. I'm glad, on the whole, that I didn't.

"Well, when I came there the next morning, I found two things that were wrong. Why should Scoville have arsenic in his tooth-powder box? The explanation appeared the next day.

"And in the second place, the soft velvet pile of the rug, which Scoville and a visitor had walked on that evening, had no marks on it except those made by the feet of policemen. It was clear, of course, that the marks had been removed. Scoville would hardly have bothered to do so if he was about to take his life.

"As for Mimi Dean, two things were too obvious. If it had been Scoville, he would not have left the arsenic in his medicine-chest, he would have thrown it down the bowl. And he would not have sent someone to buy the chocolates, and someone to take them: he would have bought and taken them himself."

Lewis paused. For the first time the painful silence was broken. Davidson's large frame moved uneasily in the chair in which he had finally sat down; and Dr. Norland shifted his bulky figure and trumpeted like a wounded elephant.

"I won't have it, sir!" he shouted. "Damme, I won't!"

"I'm afraid you'll have to, Eric," Lord Chiltern said. His voice was sharply staccato, more like itself than I remembered for days. "You've done all you could hope to do."

"I don't object to anyone's killing Nelson Scoville," Lewis continued, ignoring the interruption. "I don't like the use of poison — though, in a sense, poison was too good for her. I think if I had such a daughter, I should have done much the same thing. Only, I should have done it years ago, Lord Chiltern."

The old lord bowed his head.

"I've no proof you've done it," Lewis went on placidly. "I can't take any action about it. Dr. Norland cannot speak, although I suspect you told him the whole thing as a friend, not as a confessor."

Dr. Norland raised a great hand.

"Sir," he said, "if necessary, I should go into any court in the land, and swear that Lord Chiltern was in my house Tuesday night."

Lewis bowed gravely. "Davidson," he continued, "who saw you, I think, Lord Chiltern, at Moreton Gardens, when he went back, half-crazy,

to try to persuade Mrs. Scoville to leave the house
with him that very night, will perhaps take the
same attitude. You may have saved him from doing it himself. Ronald will soon forget that he
saw you take some sugar that one gives birds, to
make them sleep, from Mr. Maitland-Rice's table.
Braithwaite cannot be made to give evidence that
would incriminate himself.

"And therefore, as I say, it would be foolish for
anyone to give me what might be considered a confession. I fancy, to close the matter, and complete
my report to you, that you decided to do it after
Dr. Norland had told you what Thomas had told
him, that Scoville was planning to leave the
country. And perhaps even more important was
Lord Scoville's asking your advice about the old
lord's book. He was a little puzzled, and with
some reason, over what he could make of his
brother. He told you then that according to his
father's notes, Nelson Scoville had been taken from
the side of his dead mother in the cellar of an opium
den in Deptford. He was two days old, and no
one knew his father. He might be called the old
lord's most daring experiment.

"Shall we join the ladies ?"

CHAPTER TWENTY-SIX

LEWIS and I went back to town the next day.

"You don't have to come along with me, Braithwaite," he said, "if you'd rather go another way. I've had to keep you with me for fear you'd do something indiscreet. I'm afraid it's been a strain on you."

"You've puzzled me very much," I said. I was considerably subdued.

"It was all simple. I told you the way we caught criminals — when we do catch them — is by waiting for them to add something, or take something away, from the picture. You added something when you dragged out the picture of Scoville shooting. You should have left me to find it out for myself. I would have done it, sooner or later. His golf clubs, for instance, were there in his closet. I would have got around to them some time. And if you were fond of Mrs. Scoville, you'd hardly have kept the picture of her sitting on the boulder near a successful and loathed rival. But you are in love with her — pardon my having noticed it — and *ergo,* you had the picture for some other purpose. Besides, the magazine was much too clean. I was surprised it was so far out of reach, until it occurred to me you'd planted it on me."

I couldn't think of very much to say.

"What shall you do ?" I asked, as casually as I could.

"Nothing. Lord Chiltern hasn't long to live. Angina will put the black cap on for him soon, I'm afraid. He's a very old man, far older today than he was last Monday week. I had a talk with him. It's a punishment for his pride, he says. He'd re- fused to sell the diamond, the land, the furniture, but he'd sold his daughter.

"There's one thing I don't like about it at all. I told him I should tell you about it. I couldn't get up courage to tell them all."

I waited for what was blacker than what we had all heard.

"Thomas, or Elmer Wilson, didn't blackmail Scoville and Miss Dean. It was Lord Chiltern. Oh, there's no question about it; and I daresay you'll regard it as a professional secret. Lord Chil- tern felt, I suppose, that Scoville owed the Chilterns something. So he let him repair the estates. He used the room next to Scoville's when he was in town — as you know too well — and he craftily borrowed Scoville's own typewriter to write his letters on. You may remember that Elmer was taught to type at Borstal."

We stopped at the Forester's Arms for a drink. I was more shaken than I cared to own at this last information. "Then young Ronald is additionally fortunate in having Davidson for a father," I said with a shiver, picking up my pewter mug.

"Quite !" Lewis answered pleasantly, setting his down.

THE END

Milton Keynes UK
Ingram Content Group UK Ltd.
UKHW010726241123
433194UK00001B/207